Land of Hunger

A collection of short stories;
alternatively one long one

Land of Hunger

A collection of short stories;
alternatively one long one

Wayne Holloway

Winchester, UK
Washington, USA

First published by Zero Books, 2015

Zero Books is an imprint of John Hunt Publishing Ltd., Laurel House, Station Approach,
Alresford, Hants, SO24 9JH, UK
office1@jhpbooks.net
www.johnhuntpublishing.com
www.zero-books.net

For distributor details and how to order please visit the 'Ordering' section on our website.

Text copyright: Wayne Holloway 2014

ISBN: 978 1 78535 003 0
Library of Congress Control Number: 2015932360

Design: Stuart Davies

Printed and bound in the USA by Edwards Brothers Malloy

We operate a distinctive and ethical publishing philosophy in all
areas of our business, from our global network of authors to
production and worldwide distribution.

CONTENTS

Land of Hunger

1. Year Zero   1
2. If I Stop I'll Die!   7
3. A Political Education   27
4. The Earth   39
5. Friends and Work 1988–1995   67
6. Cheka Mate   81
7. Cyber Diaspora   85
8. In Country   106
9. The People's Will   112

Land of Plenty

10. The Jain Meal   121
11. Girl on a Bridge   128
12. Prefixed   135
13. Coach Class to Charlotte   145
14. SWIM/SWIY   151

Year Zero

15. Invisible Manoeuvres   164
16. King Bun   168
17. Black Flag   184

'Whosoever, in writing a modern history,
shall follow truth too near the heels may haply strike out his
teeth'
Sir Walter Raleigh, Tower of London, 1615

Dedication: Ali, always, Ali. And my friend Will for always reading and enjoying.

Year Zero

'To deprive the bourgeoisie not of its art but of its concept of art, this is the precondition of a revolutionary argument.'
Pierre Macherey, 'A Theory of Literary Production'

'I am happy to justify the actions of God's Wounds, to anybody. What we did and why we did it. From where I am hiding, (and by the way nobody will ever catch me, and if I am caught you will only have one me, there are countless thousands of us, believe you me!) all I can hear is why? Why? Why? All right then, you ask a question enough times you may just get an answer, but a bloody answer that nobody wants to fucking hear!'
Communiqué No. 1, Posted London 2010

I used to hate animals.

Well, just like most things, that's not quite true. As a kid I pestered my parents for rabbits. This went on for ages, a persistent campaign waged by me and my sister. Mum was pretty anal and didn't want them shitting on her good-as-new sofa. Dad said we wouldn't look after them, that they would be a five-minute wonder. I remember him calling lots of things I wanted when I was a kid five-minute wonders. As usual we outflanked him by way of mum, despite the sofa. His acquiescence probably earned him a blow-job.

Mum took us to the local farm where we got two rabbits, a hutch, a run, some hay and two water bottles; the whole rabbit deal.

After setting all of this up in our garden I went back inside to watch Top Cat. After a week I ignored them completely. I can't even recall their names. I do remember coming in one night from playing football in the street and finding dad cleaning out their

1

hutch. As I got myself a drink from the tap, he looked at me through the glass of the kitchen door, on his hands and knees, with his hands full of piss-soaked hay, the knees of his jeans peppered with squashed pellets of rabbit shit. He didn't say anything, just looked at me, you know, in that way they have.

As if by magic these rabbits had interpolated themselves between me and my dad. As if being friends with him wasn't hard enough, I had to feel guilty about not caring for a pair of rabbits.

I am not going to write any more about my relationship with my dad. Too boring. Think or write a few sentences about how you feel about yours. It's all the same, an endless loop taking in his relationship with his father and him with his, spiralling back to some grotty cave and two guys who didn't have anything in common except mutual disappointment. And now you got me talking about it, so enough. A little glimpse into my own sickening normality for the pages of your Fascist rags. I can see the words line up alongside the photo; a profile piece in a glossy magazine. I remember once seeing a picture of a smiling teenage Osama Bin Laden posing with family and friends on holiday in Paris. He was wearing bell-bottom jeans and had what looked like an afro. All very Seventies and laid back, which I guess was in some way ironic.

So, lies and truth in equal measure, although which is which is becoming harder to distinguish. And the photo? Shit, not that one! Add twenty years and take away twenty pounds, and please give me some facial hair, a beard, a wild Jewish or Arab beard, or a crazy Rasta one.

So why and how did I become what 'You' (cops, lawyers, journos/TV pundits/social-media commentators/sociologists) call an Anarchist? Funny that as a culture which is predicated on multiple acts of forgetting, you had to remember this word in order to call me it. As old fashioned as a Golem.

Look it up.

ANARCHIST!

A word more used to being typeset than pixelated. Class War, Crass, the Angry Brigade, almost as English as afternoon tea. Paris 1968, Astrid Proll, the Minute Men, the Spanish and Russian Civil Wars and back into history, to Thomas Muntzer and his Anabaptist rebellion; scary stories from the past, Capitalism's bogeyman, and a capital bogeyman, nemesis of fat cats priests, landlords and socialist bureaucrats alike. But also a comic book adversary, a quaint antagonist.

Even before 9/11 Anarchism had become anachronistic; a fading European folk memory, an echo from the past, from the old country. Yet traces of it were still visible in odd places; for example the character 'Bombe Voyage' in the first *Incredibles* movie. A computer-generated presence that traces a fragile line of association, however etiolated, back to the 'People's Will' Anarchist Assassins of Tzar Alexander 2 of Russia, even back to the Paris Commune, to Louis-Auguste Blanqui and the Sans-culottes. For 'Bombe Voyage' is nothing if not French...

A graphic novel antagonist, a live-action Superbomberman whose hat always cast a shadow over his features, rendering him inscrutable, hunched over as he clutches black grapefruit-shaped bombs with fizzing fuses, and chucks them willy-nilly from the shadows. Shadows that are now (over)populated by more modern adversaries who disguise themselves accordingly. Anarchist Fedoras and Taliban beards both have something to hide, not least a burning anger, revealed also by the ululating Zaghrata of Algerian women crowding the streets and souks of Pontecorvo's 'Battle of Algiers' as a wall of sound of resistance: 'Ulalalalala...'

'Purdah!' shouted with the same patois verve as the Rasta refrain 'Murdah!'

But now my tenuous liminality sounds like the ravings of the university lecturer I could have, perhaps should have, become. So enough.

The more I studied, the more apparent it became that Anarchism scores the composition of history as a funky bass-line, albeit intermittent, underneath the higher political notes of the last five-hundred years. Anarchistic in its haphazard appearances, with outbreaks in Europe and the Americas, becoming a fashionable counter-cultural symbol, a bit like the signifier 'Che Guevara' on T-shirts and button badges, not meaning much more than a nebulous anti-authoritarian set of ideas and images that won't go away but at the same time don't really coalesce into anything tangible. Anarchism is a waste product of our conformity, a constantly thwarted return of the repressed, always returning, always being repressed.

'Omnia sunt communia' it cries from off stage and we all shout 'Behind you!' from the stalls.

By the end of the twentieth century Communism and Fascism had been reworked into an obscene nostalgia for an understandable evil. A fratricidal falling out between ourselves, a century which, although managing to kill millions of citizens in innumerably terrible ways, was at least our century, and a slaughter of our making. The early years of the twenty-first century saw the appearance and immediate demonisation of the fundamentalist Muslim suicide bomber, more 'other' than any Bolsheviki, any Einsatzgruppen storm trooper, any Anarchist, more 'other' than any concentration camp guard following orders or taking photographs. We seek to deny them the spectacle of their own actions yet variously recount as near fairy story the storming of the Winter Palace (literally it was a fairy story), the selfless heroism of the International Brigades during the Spanish Civil war, the resilience of the Red Army at Stalingrad, the seductive evil of the SS, the equally mythic tale of the 'good German', the Stern gang and the creation of the state of Israel and on and on. All of this was cosa nostra, our thing. Islam is exterior to it, we forced it out at the end of the fifteenth century and now resent its return. It's as if the shock and humiliation of hosting Muslim Civilisation in Europe is only now being paid back and then some. We had to either destroy all our Alhambra's or re-appropriate them. Everything else was *Outremer*. For that was the moment when their otherness threatened to obliterate all boundaries between us and them. And we would become them which is worse than them becoming us. Neither of which would ever do. So we unfurl the crusader flag one more time, and it snaps in the hot breath of our fear...

The slaughter at Antioch, Tyre, Alexandria and Jerusalem. Jews, Muslims and Christians pyre high, goading us on from the pages of our shared history.

Even the Palestinian hijackings of the Seventies, parsed through the saturated early colour-TV footage of contemporary newsreels, belong to a nostalgia for the time, for the games of war that we played then, in contrast to now, when we are bombarded with random irruptions of third-world violence shot in high definition or captured on smartphones. Somali pirates plying the Mediterranean in search of the wealthy gin palaces and yachts of the European nouveau riche and haute bourgeoisie. The harrying of Greek island ports and Sardinian islets not seen since the fifteenth century. And all this shot by us and by them, for news or for proof of life ransom demand; blurred footage, punctuated by the inevitable glitches and drop out affecting an unsettling low-budget-horror-movie ambience.

Or crisp, military-grade raw satellite imagery delivered top down like computer-game footage but plagued by pixel drop out, lines of image literally stripped from our screens, gouging black strings reminiscent of the abyss that lurks between and behind our hallowed computer code, a contingent image which only serves to heighten our anxiety. Uploaded HD, high-tech news feeds that we bounce into space first before downloading as bad news. This is a reality that has not had time to age, let alone age well. Which is what NOW is all about, I guess.

So you see I had to make this new Anarchist at once *'us'* and at the same time also radically *'them'*. If I could close this circuit, we could leap into the future together. Until then I was cast as a romantic anachronism from the past, far from the Anarchist citizen of the future I wished to be. What was to start as nostalgia, a childish obsession, a hankering after the certainties of the twentieth century (only certain because it was over), developed into my own little war, a line in the sand that was definitely drawn in the past, yet a line that was to run onward into the future.

Even as we succumb to the next liberal/fundamentalist atrocity or mind-numbing bout of celebrity-/consumer-led economic Bacchanalia, glimpsing this word on the pages of the Daily Shite still has some resonance. On top of all exterior threats and atrocities, and against a background of accumulating ecological disaster and anxiety, what we did must have felt like a stab to the heart from within, a little punk reminder of its near anagram, ANTICHRIST!

Mustn't it?

For isn't it the betrayal of *'us'* I am really after, ripping a bloodied Christ off the cross before he dies in order to berate him, even convert him?

Years later I find myself a hunted man. I have aliases, I have killed, yet am a hero to thousands.

None of this had anything to do with my fucking parents that's for sure. I was a changeling child. The result of an incubator juggling contest played by underpaid nurses and bored hospital porters. This was the spectacle of my prematurity! Two weeks early and about a hundred years too late. Hah!

Nobody in my family had ever gone to either university or prison. I was to be the first.

If I Stop I'll Die!

'Conversation (in Yiddish) after the first burning of the town of Brody, near Lemberg, by Russians, at the outbreak of WW1:
Man: "How come your cottage escaped the fire?"
Old man: "Perhaps a miracle, heaven granted us a place to starve to death."'
From Joseph Roth, **The Wandering Jews 1927**

There are no records of my birth extant. This small detail has always, and more so now as an old man with time on his hands, irked me. It shouldn't really matter, a terribly bourgeois concern in fact, one's birthday, but the fact of its absence is like an unwanted birthmark, to which one's hand gravitates in order to touch or scratch involuntarily.

Yet the fact remains, I was born circa 1900 in a town of many names depending on when and who you talk to.

Lemberg, district capital of Eastern Galicia, a town of 160,000 souls, which was then and had been since 1773 part of the Austro-Hungarian Empire. At one time it had also been called Leopol(is), but by who I don't remember. Poles called it Lviv, Ukrainians Lvov. Like a Jewish joke. As I write it is part of the Ukrainian Soviet Socialist Republic. A town that was always lucky/unlucky enough to exist at the confluence of many ethnic and nationalist dreams, along the fault line of various political realities.

I appear in the census of 1903, a Jewish subject of the dual monarchy. The word census as ominous then as it had been in ancient Judea; Poles, Jews, Ukrainians, Greeks, Arabs, Russians, to be totted up, numbers in an unseen, but no less impending, lottery, whose tickets would eventually be punched by the clacking machines of IBM.

Years later a prison psychologist told me that my mind had

7

thrown a blanket over the details of my nativity. Forgetting my birthday is somehow wilful on my part and begs the question what else have I conveniently thrown a blanket over? How easy it is to play the language games of these psychologists!

These things I know. Details that quickly dissemble themselves into something more and at the same time less than fact. Notes swiftly woven into the early music of my life. My family came from Russia in 1880 as part of the mass exodus of Jews following the assassination of Alexander the second by an Anarchist group calling itself the 'People's Will'. Only one of the eight arrested assassins was Jewish, but that was enough to spread the fear of pogroms throughout the country amongst Jews, and a desire for vengeance born out of fear/hatred of Jews amongst the rest; the pogroms themselves swiftly followed, as surely as a dog will root out the smell of his master's shirt.

My grandfather, Mordechai, owned a soap factory in Moscow. His wife Rakhil, my grandmother, was a book keeper. Apparently, and this is third-hand family myth, he got punched in the face on his way to work. A random act of violence by a passerby just outside the factory gates. Punched to the ground and his fur coat taken from his back. Some of his workers saw what had happened and jeered him as he got to his feet. In his pocket, although he doesn't realise it yet, his gold fob watch is broken, its glass crushed under him, the hands stopped at 8.30, where they will remain for, well, that's the time the watch still tells today.

'From the windows they leaned out and laughed in my face, my own employees, like it was a holiday. Nothing I had done, or who I was, mattered. I was just a Jew who had fallen over, to be laughed at.'

He didn't go into work that day, or indeed ever again. The manic laughter that accompanies such violence was a warning:

'Beware the Pogromist!'

When he arrived in Lvov, he was lucky to get a job stocktaking in a local Brickworks. Relieved in some way to be just a Jew again without the deception of wealth and status, he saw no irony in this reversal, but it was as if the fur coat he had worn was stitched with the fabric of his soul, for he was half the man he had been just weeks before. He kept his broken watch, and took it out as often as he would when it was working, his thumb rubbing the polished back for comfort.

My father was not so fortunate. He had been studying agronomy in Moscow, but now found himself at twenty with no prospect of finishing his studies, lucky to get taken on as a day labourer on one of the many new civic building sites of this up-and-coming metropolis. There were street corners where men gathered in the hope of a day's work, shivering in the cold under clouds of tobacco smoke, carpenters, bricklayers, plasterers and ex-students. The foreman jumping down from his truck or cart would grab hands, looking for the signs of graft, taking the calloused, rejecting the lily-white.

'...you, you and you, that's it for today, come back tomorrow.'

Up into the flatbed for the lucky, the rest left to skulk back home, surplus to that day's requirements.

Ten years later Mordechai received some money from one of his old partners, I think out of guilt, I can't remember the details, so he stopped working. With that money all the memories flooded back, as if he had been punched in the face all over again. Which meant he drank and ate too much. He developed a grudge against the world, the type of grudge you can't ever satisfy, it being so general. That single punch to the face (twice delivered) proved to be his undoing. Such a little thing, but such an earth-shattering revelation for Mordechai, a moment of sheer vertiginous horror, a sundering of the curtain, the moment he became uninsured, his beloved capitalism reduced to so much chaff on the wind.

His pride curdled and there were days when Rakhil had to throw things at him just to get him out of the apartment.

Sometime later he died behind the counter of a sweetshop. A shop he had bought in order to place a counter between himself and the world. I know this because the new owner told me so. He rapped his knuckles on wood as he spoke, showing me where each of them had sat. My grandmother sold the shop because she couldn't bear to be alone behind the counter, where they had both perched, sipped tea and argued over the newspapers.

The new owner would always give me free sweets, small handfuls pushed across the counter. Free sweets! My favourites were the 'Sour Susans', named by us in honour of the old washer-woman who used to be a prostitute before she became too sour and fell on hard times. Sucking on them made the roof of my mouth sting, the pleasure of the blood-taste of iron and salt flooding my tongue.

A quarter of the town was Jewish, but my father married a gentile, a Pole. He had seen what flight had done to his father and wanted to make sure we never had to go anywhere again. The full horror of a pogrom is the fact that it is the same as being 'put to flight' in Biblical times. Thousands of years in which nothing has changed and Civilisation in toto reveals itself as one big lie for the Jews. So he, this latter-day Samson, would try and anchor us in this place, as much a temporal effort as a geographic one.

On a more prosaic level seeing his father actually working in a factory, instead of owning one, may have irked my father, whose indolent (studying agronomy? A Jew, I ask you!) Moscow life had gone up in smoke. Even amongst so many Jews, he felt a need for tenure. A Polish wife would secure this. This logic held for seventeen years.

He finally got a job working for a seed merchant, a zealot for importing newfangled crop strains of Rye and Wheat, exhorting shorter harvest cycles and double yields. He took my mother into the outlying villages and they sold seeds from the back of a covered wagon. She would interpret for him, and probably her presence reassured the peasants. She must have spoken

Ukrainian as well as Polish and probably some Russian. They had a son, Anton, my brother, who became a skilled stone mason by the age of fifteen. You see Lvov had aspirations as the century turned. And why not?

My brother died of Tuberculosis after laying what I like to believe was the final keystone of the Ivan Franko Opera house, completed in June 1900, quite possibly the year of my birth, and still standing today as far as I know. I was a late surprise. So much so my mother died giving birth to me. I was what the Germans later called 'Mischlinge', a half Jew, a cross breed. My father inherited the sweetshop, and promptly sold it, moving back in with his mother so she could take care of me. He tried to drink himself to death but the money ran out first, so he got a job working in a bar.

In 1908 my father was killed in a fight with a Pole. He died because of a woman, and in a bar too. He may or may not have been drunk, but his death would have pleased him because he wasn't killed for who he was, (a Russian Jew), but for what he did, fucking another man's wife.

See his logic of survival was illogical. Looking back it's obvious. But even at the time the odds were stacked against him and his Chutzpah. To think you could rinse out who you were, simply launder your identity, was as crazy then as it is now.

'That's why I married a Pole!' was what he used to shout at his mother, drunk, stabbing his finger in my direction.

My grandmother died shortly after my father, I don't think she had the energy left to bring me up. I was eight. What little money she had saved was given to the Elders to pay for my keep and education. I also inherited my grandfather's broken watch. I hated the family that moved into our house, but it was eventually to kill all of them. Number 43 Kresowa Street, the only family address I have ever known. Forty years later this street became the northern boundary of the final Jewish ghetto in the city, a city in which only 3000 of 100,000 Jewish inhabitants were to survive. Not me, I wasn't there, but they were.

Death came in many guises, and stalked all of us in those years, so that you see when war came it was to be just another way of dying, to go with all the others, including the Jewish way of death that has so come to dominate our minds since. The point I want to make here, at the outset, is that I don't want to retrospectively add my dead family to the wrong pile.

I'm my father's son after all and it's important to see things clearly. I want to negotiate the different piles of dead in my life, of which there are many, with a brutal honesty.

I seem to have rushed the telling of the lives and deaths of my family, using the conventional punctuation of the Holocaust to round off the story. Whether this is because I am an unconstrained egoist who wants to talk solely of himself and his exploits and has to sketch this family stuff in for sake of form I don't know. In my mind I spend a lot of time making up who these people were and indeed how much they would have loved me and I them, if things had been different. This make-believe world comforted me but I see no reason to share it with you, not just because it isn't true, for that is beside the point, but because it is not something that bears the scrutiny of being written down. In fact I started to write a journal from when I was about thirteen, which was always in my mind addressed to them, an obvious device to keep them alive and one that helped me frame my early life. Most of these notebooks are lost, burnt, scattered amongst the ruins of the things I wrote about. What I have left are referenced here, an aide to memory, re-inscribed onto the hard unforgiving surface of the present day.

As a kid I was called Buba. Buba Sobelson. Hardly original, like calling a cat puss. A street name, a throwaway name. Since then I have had many names, each one containing a clue, an echo of the one before. Finally all that is left is the letter B, a remnant, a stub, a stubborn remainder which has suited me just fine these forty odd years, and one I can promise you will be present at least on my death certificate, alongside a question mark no doubt. B. A pair of tits drawn from above. For who knows, and I mention it again (as the psychologists will tell you, I shall return to this absence again and again, worrying it like a dried scab), who knows what was written, or when, on my birth certificate? That went up in flames along with everything and everyone else so many years later.

An actual record. A death certificate. A full stop on all of this unraveling. A final hurdle, the way out of the maze, my landing on the moon. One small schlep for Yiddishkeit. In old age my mind frets over jokes and wordplay, a sign surely of my imminent demise.

I lived in the house of an old aunt. I have no idea whether she was a relative or not, but she took me in. I remember only the smell of mothballs and cabbage soup. A few chickens in the back yard, their shit compacted against the back step, my job to either chip it off or mop it up depending on the weather. The council paid her for my bed. My 'Mischlinge' status was overlooked or forgotten and I was treated like any other young Jewish kid growing up in this relatively prosperous and seemingly tolerant Mitteleuropean city. So against my father's wishes, wishes and plans he paid for in every way imaginable, I was back amongst his own people, and fell into step with the daily rhythms of an ancient 'chosen' way of life. What little Polish and Russian I had was eroded by Yiddish, which would have been 'Einer shande' if my father had lived to hear it, 'Abi me liebt' and he didn't, so.

Before the war the city was cosmopolitan. We had Russians, Jews, Poles, Ukrainians, Greeks, even the odd Muslim. Business was booming, trade, civil building works, light and heavy industry all provided jobs for a growing urban working class. Peasants from the surrounding countryside would pour into the city on market days selling meat and vegetables. They would spend the money on things for the home; pots and pans, linen, tobacco, furniture, or things from the factories, machine oils, tool parts, shoes, wire, glass, saddles, candles; they would even pose for photographs and visit restaurants on high holidays and feast days.

There was no ghetto wall, no boundary between Jewish Lvov and the rest of the city, one simply bled into the other. A Shtetl of sorts existed within the wider city, but as a communal idea more than a physical space. The boundaries in our minds had more to do with rich and poor than Jew and Gentile.

Indeed it was the rich Jews who provoked most of our jealousy because they lived nearer us than the rich Poles or Ukrainians. What I'm trying to conjure here is that Lvov before the first World War was a modern city with a cathedral, traffic jams, trams, synagogues, universities, technical colleges, factories, hair salons, VD clinics, music recitals, pickpockets, teaching hospitals, as well as poverty, crime, and what is now flagged with so much fanfare, racism.

The point of these recollections, which come thick and fast but as sense memory only, fleeting tendrils of smell, daubs of colour and flashes of movement, word, taste and temperature, is that they still refuse to be condemned, in the light of what came after. Lazy historians see the mass migration of Jews to America before WW1 as somehow marking the cities of Eastern Europe for death and destruction, black crosses daubed on so many plague doors. Condemned before I was born? Far from it. I can smell the roasting coffee from the factory on Rappaporta Street, I can hear the gypsy songs on the Ploshcha Rynok, their lime-green shawls and canary-yellow headscarfs fluttering in the breeze, their exotic musk and sun-darkened skins.

I can still taste my first kiss. A gypsy girl up against an old tree high up on Castle hill, I was thirteen, she maybe fourteen, her hot spicy tongue ran so deep into my mouth I came down my leg and she laughed in my face, spat on the ground and ran away. There we have it, my mystery, a half Jew, a gypsy girl, like in a bloody Gogol short story or one by Pushkin, or Lermontov, one of those fellows but with shame and cum and hot tears. Bark scrapes down my back, the red and green of blood and moss smearing my shirt.

I stared down at the square, trying to spy her, where Gypsies now play Django Rheinhart ditties for coins spread out on a grimy blanket from the deep sweaty pockets of incredulous American tourists; wary, forewarned tourists, husbanding their fat wallets in bum bags.

Hollow-legged and light-headed I stumbled back down the hill into the busy streets of the old town. I can see the shiny new automobiles of the city's nouveau riche, the bourgeoisie gathering on the steps of the opera house on balmy summer nights and all this in vivid colour. I can see it. I went home and picked the dried spunk from my sparse pubic hair.

When they burnt Brody in 1914, the Russians renamed the broken streets with shiny new tin signs, after Pushkin, Lermontov, Gogol, Turgenev. Their great bloody authors mocking us in our ruins with their greatness.

That little minx did steal my heart, which she burnt, but in return she gave me the gift and burden of recollection. Now, finally, an exquisite tragedy worthy of Gogol, of Chekov. I never saw her again, and as with everyone else I assume the worst instead of wondering what became of her.

So don't consign me to the ghetto conjured by your mind's eye, don't enlist me into the ranks of the walking dead, an army conscripted in your morbid late-century imagination, plagued by guilt for something that in 1910 had yet to happen. A misplaced sympathy that clouds judgement and bleeds dry the very lives I wish to remember. That I wish to bring back to life, to re-animate with blood, the sinews and flesh, warm rosy cheeks and slapped thighs, the arses and calf muscles of my family and so many others. Taste them, these wafers of life, for they are my fathers, my sons and my holy ghosts.

We were always hungry. Growing kids constantly in need of

sustenance, the aches and pains of our bodies soothed by daydreams of chops and treacle. And we would steal to feed this hunger. There were ten of us pickpockets and we styled ourselves the Gold Flag gang, after an infamous Jewish robber gang in Vilna. From St. Anne's church we ranged up and down Grodecka Street, past the pharmacist at 87, where the middle classes bought their unctions. One of us tripped them up, the others pounced like cats, shameful but easy pickings.

My best friend Leopold Weiss and I, Leo with the unbrushable red wire wool hair, who later became a famous Muslim scholar, and changed his name to Mohammed Assad (another story and I will tell it, but not here), would stalk the fat greedy peasants as they came into our neighbourhood looking to sell vegetables, mutton, sides of beef, for prices only the elders and merchants could afford. The others were younger, seven, eight years old, who loved the game of it but in some ways felt the hunger more keenly than we did, us who at ten could rationalise a little this world of haves and have nots. On our street we could boast only one 'double chin', a person who could afford enough to eat. It was rumoured that she had taken a goyim, a peasant, as her lover and probably eaten his pork into the bargain!

One farmer I remember. He was clumsy and slothful, and came from the nearby village of Slavsko. To my hungry eyes he always looked like he had just eaten a huge meal and was finding it hard to shrug it off. His two daughters on the other hand were pretty and would sit on the cart peering down at us dodging in and out of the way in an attempt to show off. Maybe my father was right about Polish women, for this troll of a peasant had managed to give birth to not one but two princesses! Sometimes they threw sweets down to us. I had no more use for them, only people who ate well liked sweets, or little children, so I made a show of giving them to the younger kids, a ridiculous man-child Pharaoh handing out gifts with exaggerated magnanimity.

The farmer would work from the back of the cart showing his

meats and barrels of vegetables. A few of our boys would run behind collecting the manure to sell as fertiliser.

Not us! Leo and I would wait until the cart stopped in front of the old synagogue. The peasant and the Rabbi argued prices but also shared a love of eating, which would pepper their haggling with exclamations of delight over some dish they both had tasted (but never together, they would never share the same table, this Jew, this Catholic, they shared only the street), indeed the porch of the synagogue was their table and the wooden side door framed this inside out friendship, the Rabbi fondling the marbling of a proffered side of beef, or nodding appreciably at a carcass of mutton in the thin spring light. At this moment of Holy Communion we pounced, the girls giggling and screaming as we upturned a few barrels and stole off with whatever we could carry.

The last time we tried it he arrived without his daughters, which should have tipped us off. He got down from the cart and went over to the side door of the synagogue. Leo jumped in as I kept watch. A roar erupted as he was grabbed from under a tarpaulin by a huge youth who we later found out was the girls' older brother. We'd never seen him before, this secret weapon. I was rooted to the spot with fear, Leo was probably being butchered in there! The peasants and the Rabbi roared with laughter, we had fallen into their trap.

I summoned the courage to peer inside to see what had become of Leo. He was sprawled face-to-face with a dead pig, diplomatically hidden at the back of the cart for want of not offending the sensibilities of valued customers, but destined for a very lucrative end in the Ukrainian neighbourhood beyond Zamarstynovska Street. A pig! And Leopold was nose-to-snout with it. The fat boy threw him out of the wagon, and before I could move, run, he jumped down, grabbed me, slapped my face and kicked me down there street after him. Tears filled my eyes and his abuse and laughter rang in my ears. I swear to this day his conversion to Islam many years later can be attributed in no small part to this shock, that and the shame of seeing the Rabbi and the fat peasants doubled up in laughter at his misfortune.

Only later (always later) did I find out that the Rabbi had paid for the food we stole, otherwise we would have been more soundly beaten. He had brokered our escape.

Aspects of life were still hidden from us. We were children after all. These peasants mocking us with their self-assured bellows, which hurt me more than any sore arse, this laughter hid a threat that ran counter to the humour. Not so many years later when villages across Russia were holding the towns to ransom for their grain I remembered this veiled fist, and the memory of it steeled me.

For wasn't this the same laughter, the same bared teeth, that spooked my grandfather into fleeing Russia all those years before?

When I was fourteen war broke out. Two hundred odd years of prosperity up in smoke. My father would have wept, all his big-city ideas fled in an instant. Austrians, Poles, Ukrainians, Russians at each other's throats overnight.

Like my grandfather I had developed a certain apprehension, I always felt things could turn against whatever small fortune I was enjoying at the time. School was like this, the street certainly was ringing with the contingent 'Now!' of childhood. As for the countryside, forget it. Open spaces scared me. I was always ready to move, to hide. Us Jews were like schools of fish, running from one shark to the next, backing themselves up into every opportune rock cave, catching their breath, until they mistook their continued existence for safety and poked their heads out into the open sea once more. If the shark didn't get them, an eel, an octopus, certainly would. And we were always, eventually, winkled out into open water.

The Russian army occupied Lvov for ten months. Thousands of Jews fled, then returned as the Hapsburgs took it back when the Russian army retreated in disarray; as the Germans said in the papers, a disorganised, badly equipped rabble, and this as a sop to the city's Jews, a Jew-hating rabble at that. But wasn't I partly Russian too? Many of the soldiers had seemed no different to the armed Catholics who ran around my City, equally but not more dangerous. What was different was some of the newspapers they read, and the loud and sometimes violent meetings they held in our public spaces. Leopold and I would listen and with our pidgin Russian make out just how hungry and unhappy these men were. Their officers were like the Austrians and Germans we'd had in Lvov since I was born, high and mighty, suspiciously clean with polished boots and shiny spurs that seemed never to touch the ground. Have you ever felt one of these shiny spurred boots pass you by at ear height? The walking pace of a war horse is the drunken swagger of a giant. The boot will veer towards you with the roll of the animal's hips, in and out, side to side, as you dance together down the street. And there you are squeezed between a wall and the hunting leather of a dragoon or cossack. The hairs on your neck stand up as you will yourself to look ahead, refusing an animal desire to look to the side or behind you, to measure the source of your fear. A fear of cold steel. Instead you smell the clean tang of polish riding the deeper sweat and shit smell of the horse, and hear the clink of sabre, and the creaking of strap and tack. You press on in the hope that they will pass, a moment impossibly delayed, until out of the corner of your eye you glimpse a spur pushing back into the horses' flank and they move past and you can breathe freely again.

That was what it was like, the ever-presence of violence, the smell of fire, shouting, the movement of horses; the multi-sensory experience of war, occupation and nationalism!

There were demonstrations and riots against the occupying German forces throughout 1915/16. When the revolution in Russia started these demonstrations intensified, soldiers rattling their guns and swords for peace and freedom. Widows and orphans, families of dead soldiers, led us in our demands for food, for only then could the rest be achieved. The local police beat us, but not mercilessly for they half agreed with our demands. But as the war dragged on and as events in Russia became more uncertain the situation in Lvov became difficult. I was a teenager, my family dead, the elders and teachers at school were no better than gaolers to my mind, stooges for the dual monarchy that was so obviously on its last legs but they were too blind to see what I, a mere child, could have painted for them in bright colours, a new dawn, a more vivid and beautiful painting than anything the bourgeois had in their precious museum on Drahomanova Street.

It was Anarchist terror that had brought my family to this city, and it would be Anarchy that chased me from it.

Peace and bread, land and freedom. An immediate ceasefire to end the Imperialist war. German, Polish, Ukrainian and Russian Peasants, Soldiers and Workers united against the landowners and the Czar. And later the cryptic 'Immediate transfer of power to the Soviets of workers, soldiers and peasants deputies!' This, excepting the last, which I didn't understand, sounded more like it. Leo and I wanted bread and we didn't want to fight and end up like the young men on the back of carts missing legs, eyes and arms, who trundled endlessly (in both directions) past our street, one day Russian, the next German or Poles.

The Hussars and Dragoons, the officers and chiefs of staff suddenly looked out of date, actors still dressed up in costume long after the show was over. These troops, these colours, this martial civilisation was swiftly going out of fashion. Lvov itself seemed more modern than the soldiers that garrisoned it. In the summer of 1917 the city etiolated in the shadow of occupation, and so did we. Early copies of Isvestia, Nasha Zarya and Rabocheyo Utro were smuggled into the city and offered tanta-lising glimpses of a distant struggle, confusing parts of a bigger picture, something more than just war weariness, but what?

Our teachers tried to protect us with diversionary tactics. Geography lessons about rain forests in South America or the formation of oxbow lakes in the Nile delta, anything about anywhere but here. That and mathematics. Increasingly complicated problems in algebra and trigonometry. We felt sorry for them, these redundant teachers. War invades the classroom and holds hostage its teachers to the history of what side are you on.

Jews didn't take sides, as they were always blamed by each side for taking the other side, so why bother. We didn't have anything to gain by this war, or indeed any war. War provided an excuse to punish us, the surfeit of anger and violence that all wars produced usually falling on our shoulders. How can you ward off an almost-mass psychological excess, something generated by the very process of living?

The revolution in Russia was going to put a stop to all that. Why, look at all the Jews involved. My fingers hungrily smudged their names on pamphlets and newspapers. I was drawn to it like I had been to the gypsy girl, equally ill-equipped to deal with this new information. I was seventeen, and had hardly ever been outside the city. But which way to go and how? To the west was just more war, somewhere out there the terrible killing fields of France and Belgium that we had read about. To the east there seemed to be the promise of peace, and much more. My pen hesitates to write this now, the drag of historical irony holds me back, but in my heart I know such irony is a terse and malnourishing mistress, her hindsight a blind curse, so I press on. A very different world lay before all of us in 1917.

I had collected things for a long journey, a map of Russia, a few spare clothes, a compass, some tins of food, but they sat under my bed, a somewhat meagre challenge to my inertia. For the time being the war looked set to continue. It had a fascination all of its own. It was our collective blood sport. Like being collectively bled, we felt a soporific comfort in the rhythms of war. The whole of Europe was enchanted by death, as if re-reading the last pages of a hoary old children's fairy tale, with its comforting sense of belonging in repetition. Over and over again. Yet somebody had taken this fairy tale and scribbled in the margins, like a mad monk doodling inside the fine curlicues of his illuminated capitals, the scraps of paper in Russian, Polish, German and Ukrainian suggested not just a different ending, but a different story altogether.

Single pages nailed to telegraph posts or pasted on walls, double-page sheets picked from amongst eddies of leaves in the grubby corners of village and town squares, grubby twists of newsprint handed surreptitiously from hand to hand, and openly from trench to trench, these dream-like promises fluttered across the front, gnomic prayers to break the world-girdling iron spell.

'...We call for an immediate ceasefire. Nationalisation of all land. Land to be disposed of by local Soviets of agricultural workers and peasants deputies. Abolition of the police, the army and the bureaucracy. The arming of the people. Confiscation of all landed estates...'

A better story? Yes, it satisfied me in the way a sci-fi pot-boiler does, or a pulp western, but you can't eat words unless they are your own, another insight I was to understand only 'later'. One morning towards the end of that summer the Rabbi beckoned me into the synagogue as I passed by on my way to find piece-work at the only place hiring in town, the munitions factory. 'Pssst!' he hissed under his breath, gesturing manically with his hand. I remember this odd sound, 'Psst!' Odd coming from him and not some street kid in an alleyway trying to sell me a stolen bike. A sound stored clearly in my memory, whereas so much else is just noise.

Inside, he fumbled in his pocket as if hesitating to withdraw his hand. He had something written down on a piece of paper for me. A name and an address in Petrograd. Karel Sobelson. He told me he was my second cousin, my grandfather's brother's son, who had been clever enough to spend most of the war in Switzerland. The Rabbi had made a few enquiries, he was a member of the Russian Social Democratic Labour Party, in effect a Jewish Communist who became a Bolshevik in 1917, and changed his name to Karl Radek. It was names like his that my fingers had smudged in their excitement. My jaw hung open as the Rabbi whispered.

'Maybe a Jew like that could command a little respect from a troublesome worthless half Jew like you?'

I took out my grandfather's watch and dangled it between us, M. Sobelson, rubbed smooth, but still legible on the back, the etching carved deep into the gold. Perhaps he could. Clever old bastard! I pulled myself together, shrugged, put the watch away. Why did he care about me? His turn to shrug, he looked down at his feet, staring at his worn-out shoes. Karel's father had made him these shoes.

'You deserve better than this.' Still looking at his shoes.

We all did, I answered him cockily, stuffing the address in my pocket.

The Rabbi was old and carried the key to the synagogue on a piece of frayed string round his neck. An ancient-looking key, a platonic key that signified exactly what it was, an opener of doors. Years later in prison I read a Dylan Thomas poem which opened with the lines 'The hand that signed the paper felled the city'. It immediately reminded me of his hand, hesitating in his pocket that chilly autumn morning, before handing me the piece of paper, and then his 'Pssst!' hit me so hard I turned in my cell to see where it came from.

At the factory I told Leo and he simply nodded in silence. Up until that moment I had nowhere to go, but this name, scribbled in the old Rabbi's spidery hand, was freighted with promise, like the propaganda we had hoarded since the war began.

After work we went up Zamkova Hill to think, to watch the sunset, sensing that we looked down on Lvov for the last time.

From here the city persisted. The spires and domes of many grand churches, the cemetery, the factories, the neighbourhoods and there the roof of the Opera House my brother had built. Topped with three winged angels. As a child I had wondered which of these had carried him to heaven. Now we didn't dream of *our* escape, but were silent at the prospect of it being upon us, not so much an escape but an expulsion. Out into the world and beyond a stone's throw from the old synagogue, which had, for the first years of our lives, provided a psychological if not physical boundary to our existence.

That night the winds of change blew again across our city, this time on horseback. A detachment of Black Hundreds rode into town to harry the by-now-depleted German occupying forces. They attacked the munitions factory. These reactionary and berserk Russians shot a few sentries and beat workers with the flat of their sabres, threatening worse, burnt copies of insurrectionary texts outside the factory gates and for good measure, as they left, set fire to the synagogue. Our last sight of Lvov was backed by fire, the old Rabbi scrabbling for his dead dog in the ruins of his temple. He waved us away without recognition, his eyes already dead, disconnected from memory. Frightened, disorientated, we chased the metallic echoes of horseshoes striking the cobbles ahead of us. We ran towards death, following the Black Hundreds out of the city, heralding us eastward.

I can remember clearly the smell of fresh horse shit as we ran along Starozhydivska Street, running for its own sake, running out of the fear that if we stopped we wouldn't get one step further.

A final memory of my father. When I was three, four years old, he took me with him into the countryside in his seed wagon. It was unusual because it was my grandmother who mainly cared for me. I knew my father found it hard to spend time with me. But I can clearly see us sitting side-by-side as the cart trundled out of the city. It was late autumn and the air was full of smoke because the peasants were burning barley stubble. It smelt good. An old peasant had somehow caught fire and ran screaming past us, the back of his shirt in flames. My father jumped down, tried to help him, to put the fire out, but he shouted 'If I stop I'll die' and kept running, eventually throwing himself in the village pond.

That's how I felt that last night in Lvov, like the peasant on fire. Like I was standing still and the city was running out underneath me on a burning wheel. At seventeen one entertains the strangest of notions, but if I had stood still that night, I would have been consumed by flames.

As I ran, I thought of my father and the morning we had shared, and the only joke we ever shared, the joke of the fat peasant on fire diving into the village pond to put himself out. My father's name was Simon.

I looked up the Rabbi's name, it's there in the many books about our vanished world, but it has no place written down here, I wouldn't want to kill him with it all over again.

This messy end of war, where sides changed daily, this deadly flickering of allegiance, was the backdrop to our unheralded exit from Lvov. Within a month the Austro-Hungarian Empire collapsed and retreating German forces handed the city over to Ukrainian Nationalists. An immediate Polish uprising in the city centre kept Ukrainians and Poles busy fighting each other for months until they concluded a joint alliance against the Bolsheviks, and inevitably against the Jews. The Lvov I had known was extinguished. One war had ended, yet another was about to begin.

'Nur die kleinen Dinge im Leben sind wichtig.'
*Joseph Roth**

'Ich bin glücklich, noch einmal, um einen alten Leben beleuchten, wie es es tat so oft in den vergangenen Jahren.

Ich sehe die Soldaten, den Mörder, den Mann, der fast ermordet wurde, den auferstandenen Mann, den Gefangenen, den Wanderer.'

*Joseph Roth***

*'Only the small things in life are worth anything.'

** 'I am happy, once more, to shed an old life, like I did so often these past years. I see the soldier, the murderer, the man who was almost murdered, the resurrected man, the captive, the wanderer.'

A Political Education

University was primarily an escape from home, a functional rite of passage, a way out from the benign, yet nonetheless stifling influence of my family. In a good old-fashioned sense it was also to give me a political education and lead to my surprisingly early downfall.

Looking back, I remember the place fondly. Here are some of the people I met and the things we did, in no particular order of importance, except that dictated by age and the vagaries of recollection.

A mature student called Vaughan, probably in his early fifties. A great hulk of a man in a filthy brown trench coat with unfathomably deep pockets. I remember that coat more than his face, except that it was big, framed by planes of flesh. The coat had the sort of pockets you could (and he did) pull chickens out of. A man who went native in the grounds of the university to research a paper on Rousseau. He slept in the woods eating grubs and berries, pondering the natural state of man. You caught glimpses of him on the way to lectures, lurching between trees like a yeti. He'd come out at night, hover nervously outside the Students' Union bar, lonely and cold. He once gave me a 'goofball', an Alice in Wonderland-sized pharmaceutical pill that gave me a crash course in the radically contingent nature of time, all sense of which I lost track of for three days. Conjuring him up now with minimal effort, he develops in a photographic sense as a combination of Oliver Reed and Aleister Crowley, but without a face. His features just don't come through, my mind draws a blank.

Frenchie was a Phil Collins stoner-type who loved hot knives and would regularly burn hash/resin/opium paste between two rusty knives in order to get really fucking stoned as quickly as possible. He loved to party and reminded me of Noel Edmunds.

Smiling, confident, home-counties, middle-class edging-posh, hale and hearty. Frenchie loved women, drinking and dope, and probably has sold BMWs at some point since leaving university with a solid 2.2 (B/A Hons Business Studies). He played rugby as a youth, which had given him a dodgy knee at some point, and he had always looked forty-something years old.

If you know people for a long period of time, you can't help but project them back into the past as they are today. We have always been the age we are now, but if you think really hard it's possible to push the sliding scale back in time, glimpsing the younger version, but only for a moment, before the slide reels us back into the present. Memory people, these living shades are immortal. Forever middle-aged, our youth haunts us.

Gary Finch, a dead ringer for Tommy Steele, was studying for a postgraduate degree in military history. A Tommy Steele double from the East End, a Chelsea fan, ex and future army (more on that later), splayed teeth, face sketched by Hogarth.

Tommy Steele grew up on the same street in Bermondsey as my nan, Old Jamaica Road. His dad was a local face called Darbo Hicks. Darbo would come into my great grandfather's pub, the Lilliput, AKA the 'Lil', and ask, (as in demand) that his son be allowed to play the piano. My mind cast Gary in this role, shrunk him down to kid size in a saloon bar full of Bookies runners and longshoremen. That was him, a six-year-old Tommy, tinkling the ivories in my family boozer. Fixed smiles all round, as he croons 'It's my Mother's birthday today'.

Gary Finch used to have a budgie and would walk around campus with it on his shoulder, casually stroking its back as he went. A real hard-nut. A real hard-nut's sentimentality. Flash on the SS officer in Klimov's movie *Come and See*, petting a marmoset perched on his shoulder as his troops run amok in a Belorussian village, feeding it nuts as the villagers are rounded up in the barn and set on fire. This sentimental/evil dichotomy has become a trope of the Holocaust in literature, of Nazi behaviour, of evil men in general. Caligula was another one. I don't think the officer actually fed the marmoset nuts in the film, he may have, but you get the picture. Gary's dad was a sergeant in the British army and Finchy, (of course we called him that), got expelled from France after a ruckus whilst on a canoeing exercise with his old man in the Ardennes.

Gary got kicked out of countries rather than schools. He was cool.

Like Vaughan he was older, a result of efforts to get more working-class people into university. We found him irresistible, even though he would get us to steal stuff, take our money at cards and generally yet genially abuse us at any opportunity. A lonely guy, estranged from his missus and child, he once whipped out his knife at a party and snipped off my braces so that my trousers fell down. Not so cool. He'd poke people in the eye for a laugh, as a way of saying 'hello mate', and this would hurt 'the mate' for the rest of the evening leaving him (invariably him) with red, weeping eyes and stinging, bruised eyeballs. His third-year thesis was on French military tactics in North Africa 1960–1965. His ambition was to use this to get him accepted into the French Foreign Legion. No word of a lie.

Why I was wearing trousers that needed braces I couldn't tell you. Finchy had a gravelly voice, same as Bill Sykes. Looking back now I would say he was a genuine, if somewhat feral, anarchist. If he had a dog it would be called Bullseye.

The Queen was to visit the University to open something. They installed a Royal convenience by the lake, a posh port-a-cabin affair. The night before the visit we rolled it into the lake.

I mean they put it right there. Campus had been full of security types in the days leading up to visit and groups of left- and right-wing students faced off over it. 'Fuck the Queen' vs 'Land of hope and glory'. The day of the visit we wanted to further disrupt events, as a follow-up to our success the night before. I remember the crush, there were snipers up on university roofs, (for fuck's sake!) yet their presence empowered us, they became our extras. By revealing their hand so strongly we felt like we had one of our own to play.

We didn't.

The Queen was doing a walkabout and we jostled someway off in the crowd, not having the courage to shout 'Piss yourself bitch' or even 'Free Nelson Mandela' to her face. Just as I was getting nearer to where she was, drawn by the magnetic vortex created by the crowd around her and without an idea or plan for what I would do next, two pairs of strong arms grabbed me and pulled me back and out of the throng, as if through an invisible curtain into another realm. Just like that. I had been extracted. Ripped from the crowd, a crowd that now was revealed as tepid, transparent, permeable, where a second earlier it had felt potent. All they said was 'Don't even think about it'. Quietly, almost politely, I had been dismissed from the historical moment. Two blokes in inconspicuous dark suits with a timeless cut, an always and never out-of-style suit, worn by faceless men who have always been right there. Army or MI5. Both, neither.

I drank out on this for weeks. Me, an enemy of the state. A political. 'Lager top, yeah thanks, now where was I saying? Oh yeah. Fascist wankers...'

The main thing I discovered about politics in university was that those involved were all tossers who couldn't get any pussy, or had any demonstrable social skill in any other arena. The dregs really of college life, the pedants who loved caucuses and voting for or against motions, supporting the peoples struggle in whatever third-world country was popular that month. Their world revolved around getting elected to the Students' Union, adopting a pro-black sections motion at the University Labour club. Or whatever. These types end up on the world stage running the country, fronts for the people/companies who direct them. That's why it has to be this type of person; avatars, hollow men and women.

So what the fuck were we meant to do? To quote Charlie Manson, look at the hand we had been dealt. Redbrick, first generation to attend university, mainly Nouveau-riche or working-class backgrounds. We were products, literally, of the post-war experiment.

Too young for punk we got post punk. Pretending that we had once seen Joy Division in Amsterdam, instead we got to see New Order. A lot. Danse Society, King Kurt, The Jam, Spear of Destiny, The Teardrops. All this shot through with echoes, after-shocks of the war, parsed as Fascist/Soviet iconography. Joy Division were literally of the Holocaust, by way of post-punk posturing and modish ambiguity. We were the last effluvia of the sixties, grains on an alluvial plain, left high and dry after twenty years of dissent and direct action. We waited. We read, we drank, confident the tide of history would return and pick us up. We were full of de-construction, certain of the inability for meaning to stick with any great certainty, anywhere.

Everything was held in parentheses, which was the best excuse I could muster for indulging myself in bouts of amazing decadence. Getting pissed day after day was a cumulative project, drugs and fucking our sensualist spectacle. Heads full of the Spanish Civil War, Angola, Namibia, intense debates over Menshevik/Bolshevik positions in early Soviet Russia, we were woefully under/over-prepared for what came our way. The tide, when it eventually came in, took us by surprise.

The miners' strike of 1984–1985.

The great Punkt, the full-stop of history as we saw it, the last squeeze of the lemon. Little did we know then that time and history marches on and that a new world order lay just around the corner/over the rainbow. No, we were still mesmerised by the tragi-comedy of the twentieth century. Long after the climax of the third act, we sustained ourselves on the wrapping up of the story and stayed glued to our seats for the end credits to roll.

I remember my Communist party membership card, it was a

pinkish cardboard affair, folded, with spaces for dues stamps on the right-hand side. An Anglo-Soviet trade delegation came to campus and we got drunk with who we assumed were KGB officers, one even drank enough to muster James Bond impersonations for us; a weasely man who smoked those fucking Russian fags that look like black tampon applicators. Yellow skin, skein of smoke, black teeth. That's all I remember. That and the handshakes and the badges. I wore one that depicted in cheap plastic relief a drive past of nuclear warheads under the walls of the Kremlin.

I also have to admit to a brush with the stage. I got the part of the *Spirit of the Revolution* in Volker Braun's play 'The Great Peace'. Backstage before opening night (God forgive me) the cast agreed to drop loads of acid and fuck the whole thing up 'cos it was shit. A great idea that only I took up. My entrance in the play was to be on a garlanded swing. Let me explain. 'The Great Peace' was 'set' in ancient China, populated by a fantastical mix of worker peasants and mythological spirits. I was meant to swing over the stage and hand the hero peasant the sword of the revolution. In fact we had rehearsed this and it worked perfectly. On the night I swung, fell and flattened him. Volker was there in the front row, artistic director of Brecht's Berliner Ensemble, and Lord Muck of the East German intelligentsia, plus all the liberal press, the great and the good of our cultural elite. This was the first (and last) time the play was performed in the West. They carried me off delirious.

When I came down I was told I'd never work in the theatre again by the director who had a double-barrelled name and was also the captain of the university frisbee team.

In 1984 I had my first taste of MDMA powder, off an American friend who had it mailed to him. I can remember now its exhilarating affects, walking into the student bar feeling like John Wayne and buying everyone drinks until I fell over. Sticking our wet fingers in the envelope like sherbet dib dabs. So munted, we gibbered at the walls of our flats, spent hours stumbling a few feet in narrow halls, heads clamped in invisible vices, cocked and locked at off-kilter angles as it all surged through us.

Writing this now from the staggering years of the twenty-first century, all I am left with is the empty, meaningless perspective of hindsight. And I cry at that, I really do. The miners' strike was for me the last echo of Kronstadt, the very last of Eisenstein's steps, a chance to see in the flesh an enemy one had only read about and stand alongside allies one had vividly imagined. For the miners it was a fight for jobs. Oh what happy hubris.

At the time we believed that the British toiling masses had been deprived the fruits of a revolution by the First World War. A demonstrable and orchestrated winnowing of the European working class that allowed the British aristocracy and their underlings to man the trams eight years later during the general strike. 'Toot toot' over the top, the hated officer cowered in the trenches as the embryonic revolutionary masses impaled themselves on the bayonets of their German Brethren.

Nena's '99 Red Balloons' was No.1 in the UK charts on the day the miners' strike was called on March 12, 1984. No shit.

Ninety-nine Decision Street
Ninety-nine ministers meet
To worry, worry, super-scurry
Call the troops out in a hurry
This is what we've waited for
This is it boys, this is war
The President is on the line
As ninety-nine red balloons go by

There is a desire in all of us to romanticise, to place ourselves in a wider history, or better to place history in ourselves, to re-rack things with us as the eight-ball, from where we extend our sphere of influence. We hope. For many, especially in 1984, 'it was money wot made us famous'. For me, and others, there was something else, another banner under which to march, albeit to a war that had been won and lost fifty years before.

We, the generation that read Commando magazine and played British Bulldog in the playground. That was us at Wapping, Orgreave, Notts, Kent, Chesterfield, intoxicated by what the Americans call 'old European thinking'. Scabs and Krauts, Commies and Jews, history right here, in my ringing head as I lay curled up like a foetus, protected by a good copper's shield from the reigning blows of his colleagues batons outside News International, having chucked a bag of marbles under a police horse's feet, and then been snatched from the mob through the front row of a police surge.

'Leave it out lads, he's just a kid'

'Fucking dirty cunt, not smiling now cunt are ya?!'

'Christ!'

'Little Wanker!'

'You broke that fucking horse's leg, think that's funny? It'll have to be put down. I'll fucking break your neck!'

'Leave it out I said, fuck me, back off Dave, I'm taking him in, he's just a fucking kid'

'You fancy him or what?'

'Cunt!'

Coppers really hate it when you chuck marbles at their horse, it really winds them up.

Cut to:

A policewoman's foot on the back of my neck, after a pissed up fracas at York racetrack, involving the diminutive lead singer of Spear of Destiny in Echo and the Bunnymen's dressing room. Egged on by Pete De Freitas to call Kurt Brandon a dwarf, it was me who ended up being arrested. I remember shouting abuse up at this bitch for the miners, for what was happening across the British coalfields. A right little Lenin I was, my Zeppelin ego, manned by the heroes and villains of a century that hardly knew me, was about to burst, or more correctly be brought down in incandescent flames.

Coal lorries were ferrying scab coal from the docks to the power stations. These lorry drivers ran a blockade of striking miners and their supporters up and down the country. But some were still getting through, getting onto the motorways and away. Some of the miners thought they should be stopped no matter what. There were bridges across the roads from where we could throw concrete slabs down onto the windscreens of these lorries. So that's what I did, with a small group of others, shitting ourselves at the prospect, but nevertheless waiting in a flat dawn drizzle, watching for the lorry's approach. A slab of concrete held between me and another, a now nameable miner who died of emphysema in 2000, who that Easter morning left me on the bridge with a hard comradely punch in the face telling me he'd kill me if I got caught and told the coppers his name.

The lorry came to rest on its side a good three-hundred yards past the bridge, it had skewed past the crash barrier and ploughed into a stand of freshly planted trees. The moment the weight of concrete left my hands a terrible existential shiver came on me. The knowledge of not being able to take it back, of not having those few seconds again in which to make another decision. The second in which a parallel world is conceived fully grown and recognisable as everything up to that point but nothing beyond it, from which you are jettisoned into its nightmare future twin. The one you chose. This moment could last forever but instead the worlds abhor each other and rush apart, my new one speeding up crazily with the miner's punch, hot tears and a bloody nose, and my running off, the other one falling back to earth, the me of a minute ago become a stranger upon whom I would lavish moments of melancholic reflection for the rest of my life.

The lorry driver broke both his legs and sustained a hairline fracture to his skull. He made a full recovery but wouldn't drive again and was pensioned off. Over 100k compensation with which he drank and whored himself to death after his wife left him. Like a lottery winner, the concrete slab his winning ticket.

During the three days it took for the police to catch me I didn't know any of the details, I was so fucking drunk I even sat and watched the news reports with a smile on my face in the student bar. Imagine what it must be like to watch a news story about something terrible, knowing that it was you they were looking for. My god to carry that around. Well for two days that was me. I was literally sick to my stomach. Like being on a plane carrying condoms full of heroin in your stomach, waiting, waiting to be found out, for the tap on the shoulder, the knock at the door. This feeling of terrible inevitability would alternate with a strange euphoria. I felt the burden of my life being taken away from me. It was as if everything I had believed in and fantasised over had come true. History was now taking an interest in me, I had been noticed. Little was I to know, when they broke down my door, that history in this sense was impersonal, mundane, and overwhelmingly disinterested. It marched on, needless to say all over me.

I was still pissed from the night before, so none of it felt like it was happening. There was an ironic distance me and the events around me. The pigs were just actors on the stage, we were all playing silly buggers and I was still the fucking spirit of the revolution. And this time I remembered my lines,

'Pigs!'

'Fascists!'

'Fuckin' Filth!'

They couldn't believe it, I was just a little cunt and so full of gob, they actually hesitated before pummelling me. A few slaps in the back of the van and then at the station a good kick in followed by an interrogation. Who organised the attack? Was it sanctioned by the N.U.M.? What other actions were we planning? What group was I a member of? Known association with the

Communist party?

'Your wife sucks off the boss class.' Kapow! Smack in the mouth, 'Running dogs of etc...', Oof! Smash! In the shins, 'Queers!' Jeering laughter, boot! in the guts. You get the picture. The coppers were all into double bubble by then so it was a result all round. Lovely Jubbly.

Then the clever one came in, Detective Rowe. I can see him now. He looked like a poxy university lecturer, all dressed down, stubble, Camel boots, he even wore bloody cords; a real maverick cop, exactly like an unbelievable detective off the telly. Although his opening gambit was all too believable.

'Ten years minimum for this little lot you stupid middle-class shite. How did you get strung along by that fucking rabble? I called your old man, he was disgusted with you boy, silly little cunt, they'll fuck your arse off in the nick, and you know what? You'll deserve it, more like you'll come to love it. Now, how about you start talking, give me some names and maybe I can help you out.'

Well he nailed me with all that didn't he? Other than the minor point that I was technically lower-middle-class, that invisible class of heroes ignored by the rest, the real troopers of society, the glue...

I almost shit myself after he was done with this little speech. I got the impression that the cops knew exactly what was going on, in fact they probably had informers who told them what we were up to before we did it. But they let it happen. Remember the other guy? My punching comrade? I never told them his name, and in not doing so found a little squalid honour that was to sustain me over the months ahead. I don't know to this day whether he was a grass, or had cut a deal. Fuck him if he did, the Devil knows his own.

'Actually, technically I'm lower-middle-class...'

'Student tosser!'

Backhand across the face. I'm on the floor wiping snot and

blood out of my mouth. And so it went on, until they abruptly lost interest, and chucked me in a holding cell.

Too old to be a young offender they sent me to Ford open prison in Sussex. A threat, me? Not yet.

The Earth

(Prison Writings 1968/69)

It was late September. Leo and I travelled east. He had family in Kiev, and from there I could try and get on a train to Petrograd. Seas of people and movement of every kind. Houses turned inside out and piled onto flimsy carts, dragged by skinny ponies, cursed by indifferent peasants. Twice ragged bands of cossacks swept past us, thankfully their steel sheathed as they fled the collapsing front and ran towards home, east to the Don, south to the Kuban. A human earthquake was rolling across the Ukraine, horses, wagons, buggies, cars and trucks, the roads were full of everybody. Soldiers, Gypsies, old people, families, gangs of lost children, Jews. Crossroads were like vortices, sucking people in and spitting them out to all four points of the compass. Nobody noticed us. We stole food from the fields and picked pockets in chaotic market squares.

Everywhere there were impromptu meetings, especially at railway stations and outside post offices, where the news was the freshest. Soldiers would take the makeshift hustings, then give way to peasants and workers. Peace, Bread, Land and Freedom! The things they said pleased each other and for the first time I saw that these people could be on the same side, the plough and the sword together. Boy soldiers shook rifles above their heads as speakers promised them the earth. Dipping pockets we helped ourselves. The road was an education, it prepared me for what I was to hear in Petrograd and Moscow, as this earthquake tumbled me into Russia.

In Kiev I managed to find a train and Leopold saw me off, as I ran, skipped and lunged from the sidings up onto the last carriage. He waved in silence, clutching a piece of paper with the address of his mother's cousin; on these threads of remote possibility hung our fortunes. We never saw each other again but I read some of his books in prison and wrote him an unanswered letter.

(A homeless Jew from Lvov, who survived the September pogroms of 1919 to become a Muslim scholar! Another story seeded in that fertile year of upheaval...)

The train rushed me to my future, one bride amongst millions that fate took that year.

Petrograd, October 1917
1am

Radek my cousin treats me like a long-lost brother. He looks serious, like a Rabbi, scruffy hair and large sideburns, a cloud of smoke from his pipe follows wherever he goes, but he has a warm face with soft eyes. There is no physical resemblance between us at all. I showed him my grandfather's watch, told its story, scant proof I am who I say I am, but he took me at my word, muttering of course I am his cousin, who else could I be?

The city is bursting with people. On the streets everything is normal, trams and buses are running, schools and shops are all open. There are no Germans here, but Radek says I should not blame them, that the German soldiers are my brothers! There are so many foreigners here, and Jews who all mix in with everybody else. There are no Rabbis and lots of young women who shout like men about things Leo and I barely whispered of on top of Zarovna hill. These women dress like men too, which is disappointing.

Thousands of soldiers camp in the streets, marching and chanting and applauding speakers on every corner. The war is over for Russia, and the officers must be in hiding, none of them are here. I was inside a palace today, the life these people led, all the rooms they had...

THERE WAS A SOUP TUREEN MADE OF SILVER THAT I COULD HAVE BATHED IN!

The hunger here is the same as at home though, so when we inherit the earth I hope it means we get to eat more of it. Land, Bread and Peace remember. Hah! After being here a week I am starting to develop a revolutionary sense of humour...

Radek. My cousin the Bolsheviki. Years later an astronomer called Lubos Kohoutek had named an asteroid after him. 2375 Radek. I cried when I read that. For the first time. Prison makes you prone to sentimentality, yet usually I am steeled against it. But this 2375 Radek somehow got through my defences; his namesake in space for ever, put there by a Czech scientist with an ironic sense of both humour and history. An inter-galactic return of the repressed. Radek was to disappear in the chaos engines of the late thirties after having helped draft the new Soviet constitution in 1936. He was put on trial, then disappeared. Some say he died before the war, others claim to have seen him in Moscow in the fifties. Just the fact of this confusion, this sense of there being nothing definite, no full-stop to his life, tied him to me, who had no definite beginning. The first time I met him I was half-starved, had been robbed and beaten on that bloody train from Kiev and had arrived looking like a landless labourer from the previous century. All I had was the watch that I had hidden up my arse, with just the chain hanging out to retrieve it! His landlady directed me to a local coffeehouse. Radek, my cousin, greeted me with a loud laugh, a slap on the back and a plate of sausage which I devoured joyfully albeit with a sore arse. Maybe at another time he would have questioned me more, but on the eve of revolution the appearance of a distant relative was just something else to deal with and hopefully put to good use.

Radek introduced me to an older man in a wig whose fingers constantly worried his stubbly chin; this was Lenin in disguise, a man uncomfortable without his beard but afraid for his life on the streets of revolutionary Petrograd! As Radek's Yiddish-speaking cousin from Lvov, Lenin asked me for news of the

Ukraine and if I had participated in the local Soviet and what I thought about the defection of many Left SRs to the Bolshevik cause. Not a man for small talk this Lenin. I was speechless. Luckily he overheard something he didn't like from the table behind us, turned adroitly in his seat and barked that nobody would support Karensky's provisional government now it had decided to continue fighting. An argument broke out for and against continuing the war, those in favour seemed to have the upper hand from what I could follow, this form of debate as alien to me as speaking French.

'The imperialist war will transform itself into a revolutionary war we can spread across the whole of Europe.' This from a skinny man with a narrow serious face and pince-nez spectacles, in other words the soon to be commissar for war Leon Trotsky.

Lenin stormed out, only to storm back in again minutes later to make the point that Russia needed peace beyond and above any other consideration however revolutionary that was and that this piece of bread, which he grabbed from the table, was more important than any revolutionary sloganeering from those snug in a tavern in Petersburg. He threw the bread across the room and it hit Trotsky square in the chest.

Lenin was a stockier, more forceful man than people think, as if in another life he could have been a boilerman. I sat there nursing my drink, mesmerised by all this talking. I told them that the Ukraine was ready for revolution, that the people demanded land and peace but didn't know who to demand it from. They fell about laughing and Lenin said that the peasants and workers of the Ukraine should demand such things from themselves, that power, the power to own land and factories had passed over to the people. The table roared with a drunken cheer, and I joined in, throwing my pitifully threadbare cap to the rafters.

After Lenin had gone I told Radek why my grandfather's watch didn't work, about the punch knocking him down that day in Moscow, the day he decided to leave Russia for good. Radek looked at me, took my bony hands in his and closed them both around the old fob watch. His nose wrinkled as although I had managed to quickly wash it at his boarding house, it still stank slightly of shit.

I told him about the Rabbi, about the Cossacks. He promised that together we would take the revolution to Moscow and sweep the anti-Semites, the Black Hundreds from the country. Radek had me then, by God he had me.

Trotsky planned and pulled off what amounted to a coup d'Etat in the next weeks; his men, less than 1000 under Ovseienko, practiced taking over the city's services: post offices, telegraph offices, power stations, gas, water grain silos. This was what mattered when it came to Red October! Lenin fussed over the support of the unions, of the sailors of Kronstadt, Kerensky used his cadets and cossacks to protect the seats of government the Touride and Winter Palaces. Trotsky meanwhile ensured the capture of the state itself and not the government. That was true revolution, the occupation of public services! After this taking the Winter Palace was merely the coup de grace, the guns of the battleship Aurora joining in the ceremony, heralding the Bolsheviks into the symbolic seat of power. Cautious from years of exile Lenin would only get rid of his disguise when the storming of the symbolic victory was reported, only then did he throw away his ridiculous wig, run his hand over his formidable forehead and stride into the Smolny institute and the already in progress soviet congress an unlikely victor. He never liked Trotsky, his hot temperament shielding cold tactics, and it's hard to think what they had in common outside the ideas of revolution. Theirs was not a moral communion. It would have made both of them smile to think that when Lenin died his enemies claimed Trotsky planned to steal his body.

For the next months I was to follow them about like a lost dog. Picking up more Russian as I went and being useful in translating what little Polish and Ukrainian I knew for the party.

These men mesmerised me. Their strong passions, the numbers of people who would stand and hear them talk, the power that literally flowed from Lenin's study. And the chaos. We all had nothing. There was no cellar of wine or kitchens full of food. The cellars had all been looted, the food gone who knows where. Barley soup and third rations of bread made from oats and chaff being the staple of those days.

Handwritten side margin note:
'We' already, see a Jew's big mistake is the use of this big word. We. Hah, let's see where it takes us, where WE end up! The downfall of Trotski, much of it brought on by himself, his hatred and contempt of others who opposed him, but to see him referred to as being 'courageous as a tartar and as mean as a Jew', to see anti-Semitism once again be used against him after his victories in the civil war... This 'we' was the same as ever, a biblical tragedy.
Revised, 1980

In February 1918 the central powers launched a massive attack against the new and weak government. Lenin fled to safety in Moscow. By March the Bolsheviks had concluded a treaty with Germany, giving them amongst other concessions Lvov and most of the rest of the Ukraine. I was shocked but Radek explained to me that without an army the new Soviet government was virtually powerless. I thought these German soldiers were supposed to be my brothers, but now it seemed the bloodlust of war was about to return, indeed it had never gone away, and the fine words of revolution had to face up to the facts.

The treaty with the central powers had opened a can of worms and everybody now hankered after their independence. Freedom looked like being bloodier than Monarchy!

We arrived in Moscow and a paper revolution began, I have never seen so many orders scribbled, annotated, handed out and transcribed into what seemed a thousand languages. Out of all this paper we hoped to conjure food. Without grain the revolution would be starved out. It was that simple. Lenin called Tsar hunger his greatest enemy. Workers and soldiers were sent into the countryside to take grain at a price we could afford to pay. The banks refused our requests for money, so we took control of the banks. But most of the money had already gone south to arm our enemies.

In an office nearby Lenin's I worked for Aleksandr Tsuirupa, in the new dictatorship of food supply. My first job was hand printing maps so that the requisitioning parties could find the bloody villages. Then it was off to the factories to see if they had voted any workers into the countryside to secure grain. Our plan was to turn the poor peasants against the rich ones, supply the poor peasants with city goods, deliver them ownership of the estates, anything in return for grain. Workers were collapsing at their stations, slumped at their lathes with hunger, productivity plummeted and all this as our enemies armed themselves on all fronts.

It was here I met Anna Petrovna, a scary-looking matron in her late thirties whose job was to make sure Lenin and whoever else was in the Kremlin got up in time for meetings. She was the timekeeper of the revolution. When drunk she would pour cold water over them. Lenin himself was a big tea-drinker, so not him, but most everyone else. Cursed, threatened, but in a strange way cherished by these serious yet debauched men, Anna had free run of the place. She mothered them in a very Russian fashion, all chastisement and wry tolerance. With her I learnt about women, about the shackles of motherhood and the future freedom of womankind! Along with all this freedom I learnt about sex, discovered this other hunger in the rarified and cold air of the Kremlin. I think many of us were nourished by sex more than the ever-dwindling rations of food that came our way. God she was almost 40, but we were both hungry.

'The war against hunger is the war against the bourgeoisie carried from the city into the countryside. A dictatorship of food supply would support the poorest peasants and compel the rich, the village bourgeoisie, to surrender their huge grain reserves to the starving people of Russia.' *Pravda, May 12, 1918.*

May 15, 1918

Iaroslav province village of Laptevsko-Popovskaia. The peasants came out to the station to meet us. We assumed they were from the local committee of the poor, but our joy at seeing them quickly turned to fear as they set about our carriages with their pitchforks and sticks. There were hundreds of them penning us inside the carriages. The noise was terrible as the horses in the car behind us panicked, reared up and trampled the wooden boards. Later I saw a cavalryman crying over the dead body of his horse he had to shoot because of a broken foreleg. He was fifteen. Apparently another detachment had already been through here a few days before. We had no idea, and these peasants didn't let us explain, far from it, we were thrashed off their land, our train barely making it clear of the station.

Shots rang out and the peasants fell back, one of their number wounded if not killed. God it was a mess! In my pocket is a crumpled telegram, one of hundreds we have reproduced to show the peasants the plight of our workers.

'*Starving workers are collapsing at their machines. Everyone who is able continues to work and will continue to do so. We beg you to send us bread. This is not a threat but a final cry of despair.*'

Signed workers Soviet of Vyksa, wherever that is.

After four years of war and now hell-bent on revolution, surely we are on a journey to emancipate souls only, for how could mere bodies survive it? I spoke to a soldier who had been at the front who says we are shedding our bodies, that physical life is being snuffed out. What Lenin says is right, the Imperial/Capitalist machine blindly demands flesh, in its death rage it demands that our bodies be ground up like offal. We have to have grain! We had to burn more precious fuel to get to our next destination, which I hope we will reach tomorrow and with less opposition! The sunset is dark and bloody, the Horizon flat and endless, yet we go on.

May 16, 1918
The telegram stutters out more demands for us to succeed in our work, more black letters of despair spill out from the machine. 'We have no bread. The situation is hopeless. Hunger reigns,' is typical. I am sick of these messages now, as we trundle into the great interior of this damn country and I ache for the walls of a city, Lvov, Peter, Moscow, anywhere but these open plains, somewhere private to hide away in and die...

The villages were some miles from the railway spur, so we split up into two groups of about seventy men, each with its detachment of fifteen Red Guard cavalry. We marched to our village, me with my first rifle slung over my shoulder, a lot heavier than I thought it would be, its rust and oil smearing my tunic. We marched behind a red banner that proclaimed 'Workers and peasants unite!' A tatty homemade banner, which made us look old, worn-out already. I fear we don't have enough cloth for new ones, the workers with us from the great Prokhorov cotton mill hadn't milled any cotton for weeks. They were tough proud fellows who were starving and without work, 'So why not bash a few fat peasant heads in?' they jested, although by the look of them it wasn't a joke. The villagers met us in the small muddy square by the church. Which were the poor peasants and which the rich? We demanded to speak to the local committee of the poor but were told that there wasn't one. We asked for the grain but they said they had none. The cavalry circled the village looking for granaries. A soldier on my right clicked the safety catch off his rifle. I fumbled with mine, having been shown how to use it on the train. Sweat ran down my back, and stung my eyes.

The commissar shouted out at the top of his voice for the poor peasants of the village to fall in on his left. Another soldier had run into the church and was ringing the bell. Tough, ragged men and a few fat women started to feed into the square from the muddy streets and alleys of the village. Our mill workers started to jeer at the peasants telling them it wasn't right that workers should starve in their factories. A poor peasant with a limp, eyes lowered to the ground, came and whispered something into our commander's ear. Past the sullen mass of peasants we followed him into a huge barn where we found to our amazement little grain but hundreds of bottles of Samogen, home-brewed vodka! Fucking selfish bastards. We forced a fat one to drink a whole bottle down in one go, he threw up, collapsed, I kicked him as he crawled away. At gunpoint we forced the villagers to smash every bottle. Well, every bottle left that our men couldn't carry.

We counted enough for fifteen thousand people in a village of seven hundred. These kulak donkeys will be the end of us!

'To sit in Peter, to starve to hang around empty factories, to amuse oneself with absurd dreams, is stupid and criminal!' *Lenin, May 1918.*

'Our detachments ought to take with them a few women, proletarian mothers and wives, who know better than anyone else just what hunger means to a family where there are many children. Such toiling mothers will really give the kulaks a piece of their minds.' *Trotskii, Petrograd, May 1918.*

'Moscow needs grain. Give it to us at the official price set by

Soviet authority. Comrades! There will be grain!' *Trotskii, Moscow, Summer 1918.*

That summer the howls of outrage and pure hatred I heard from party leaders scared the hell out of me. I had returned to the city from my one requisitioning trip after two weeks exhausted. Tsuirupa was downhearted. Only comrade Kalinin in Petrograd, himself a peasant, had managed to strike a bargain with the villages under his jurisdiction. I had been happy to cajole the peasants with my rifle, and admitted so at the time, in fact I remember confessing to the commissar how easy I had found it to hate these kulaks. It chilled me when he rhetorically asked me why I thought they sent so many Jews on these detachments, if it wasn't for precisely that reason. He was right. He was also the first person to mention my Jewishness for many months.

The next village we came to I kicked in the door of a house pushing the owner ahead of me down into the cellar. When he held up yet more bottles of fucking vodka I struck him across his smirking face, knocking him down onto his damn bottles and smashing them, to the screams of his wife and children. She grabbed me from behind and I turned pushing her away from me. I raised my hand to slap her, but turned and kicked her husband instead, before stumbling up the stairs shaking and gasping for breath. I caught the eye of two comrades coming out of houses opposite and we exchanged guilty adrenalin smiles. I laughed, in horror. I struggled to choke back the rage that swelled up into the back of my throat on a tide of acids and juices, for so long neglected in my stomach. I threw up, happy for the release. Over the next months the same rage nagged at me like a persistent sore throat. There were no more journal entries for the rest of that trip, I had run out of paper. But I imagine they would have been unselfconsciously revolutionary in tone, what we would call today 'turgid party pieces'. But in fact if you weren't there, if you didn't see the look of hatred and feral greed in the eye of that peasant, his self-defeating stupidity and that of thousands others like him, or the cheering crowds of poor peasants behind the scruffy, proud handmade banners of their committees as they drove cart-loads of grain to the railway, to deliver them to the railway workers who had come with their trains to collect them, and who in turn handed out precious parcels of shoes and a commissar standing there handing out receipts and Soviet currency, if you didn't see it with your own eyes, but just read these words on a page, then who knows what was right or wrong?

Back in the city it was easier to be hungry. It was a more abstract hunger, a fact of life, and for a while my anger subsided; moreover I lost myself again in the arms of Anna, meaning we fucked ourselves into blissful oblivion whenever we could muster the energy.

August 30, 1918

I am shot! Today a woman tried to kill Lenin! One shot went through my hand the other two hit him but he lives, I think he lives! We were at the Hammer and Sickle factory, Lenin reading out comradely greetings from workers in France, Britain and Germany. There was talk of a Communist international that after the civil war would unite all the workers of the world. As we came out of the factory gates a large crowd had gathered to see what the fuss was about, to see Lenin. Hungry faces surrounded us, I was learning how to read for signs of trouble. A woman caught my eye, behind the first ranks of workers. Our Red Guards were being jostled, holding back these men. She was older and had eyes like stones. As she came towards us the crowd parted. She raised her arm. I saw her green handkerchief fall from her sleeve, it seemed to take ages to reach the ground and my eye was drawn to it. Her hand shook, the gun looked big and heavy in her bony hand. I threw myself at Lenin who was talking as ever and shaking hands in front of me, I pushed him to the ground as the shots rang out. My hands went up and I felt like I had been stung by a giant bee. The woman's face looked oddly relieved as she was knocked down by the two workers standing next to her. I wrapped my hand in her handkerchief as they took Lenin away in his Rolls Royce.

September 3
I visited Lenin in hospital, he looked at my hand and joked that I was the best news he had had from the Ukraine in a long time.

Afterwards I went to the prison, my hand still stings like hell, but I wanted to witness her statement. I wrote it down.

'My name is Fanya Kaplan. Today I tried to kill Lenin. I did it on my own. I will not say from whom I obtained my revolver. I will give no details. I had resolved to kill Lenin long ago. I consider him a traitor to the revolution. My only regret is that I failed and for that I am sorry. Long live the revolution!'

Despite what she did I feel sorry for her, she is virtually blind it seems, she squints at her interrogators, but is to be shot. A hard woman who had been in prison under the Tsars, and now Red terror is to be unleashed on the enemies of the people. We are it seems at war on all fronts.

From then on I was seen as something of a Bolshevik lucky mascot. My hand healed and I went back to work. Yet I was sick of being in the city and wanted to return home. The arrests extended beyond just cranks like Caplan, but Anarchists too had been rounded up in Moscow. I think this is why Lenin sent me with Mahkno as his personal emissary, he saw my homesickness and perhaps a little of my despair. To the others I was just a boy, and in saving Lenin I became no more a man in their eyes, rather a novelty, a fetishised good luck token.

Radek also pressed for my exit from the Kremlin, so when the gruff, fiery and altogether mesmerising Libertarian Anarchist

Nestor Mahkno came to visit Lenin and ask for his help in fighting the Whites in his native Ukraine, I was sent back with him. After my experiences that spring I wanted to make common cause with the poor peasants of my native Ukraine, and also to rid myself of the disgust I had felt since then, not all of it directed at the Kulaks and landlords.

This slight man, this Makhno was familiar to me from so many folktales and nightmares of what awaited a defenceless Jewish child outside the ghetto. Lenin had sat him down in an armchair, poured him vodka, leaving the bottle on his desk, something I had never seen before, and himself a cup of tea and proceeded to lecture him on the unsuitability of anarchism to secure the revolution! Makhno spat his vodka onto the floor. Lenin held his tongue as Mahkno reviled the Red Guard as cowards who kept themselves to the railways in their beloved armoured cars, whilst the real fighting took place in the villages. Lenin appeared shocked by this description of his forces. He called me from where I was eavesdropping next door with Sverdlov. I came in and he introduced me. 'Take him back with you, show him what you say, let him report back to me, so that we can furnish you with what you need. Let him be a token of my trust, and maybe he will be as lucky for you as he was for me. Let us make common war on the enemies of revolution today, and then see what tomorrow brings between us.'

Mahkno needed arms, Lenin needed all the help he could get until Trotsky had got the Red Army into shape. This was their common ground. My relationship with Mahkno was to exist in this space, born out of this cooperation. Indeed my identity, my beliefs and my manhood were forged in that margin even as it was whittled away to nothing.

He stared suspiciously at my scarred hand before shaking it. Lenin laughed.

Again I was to be an emblem, a representative of this fragile alliance. And if it should fail, then what would become of me?

Mahkno was probably only ten years older than I, definitely no more than thirty, surprisingly slight in build, his personality stolen from a much bigger man. A peasant from the small southern Ukrainian town of Gulyai-Polye, in which he had established a libertarian commune as early as March 1917, less than a month after having been freed from Burkya prison in Moscow. He had fought and organised against feudal land owners, Russian administrators, police informers and factory bosses since the 1905 revolution, during which he took part in anarchist organisations, terrorist insurrections and political assassinations until his arrest for murdering a policeman in 1909. Like the Bolsheviks he believed in bread, land and freedom and above all peace, but unlike them his beliefs came directly from his lived experience as a peasant under landowners. The way these pigs rode roughshod over the people I knew only too well from Lvov, and from what I had seen in Iaroslav province. In fact one of the first things I learnt about Mahkno was that he had organised an exchange of grain for shoes and clothes between Gulyai-Polye and the workers of a factory in Ekatorinoslav. This was a cleaner revolution! And I longed to cleanse myself in it. In the remote villages of Eastern Ukraine, you could feel tangibly the removal of generations of exploitation, of physical intimidation that the communes, the free soviets, brought to the people. They had lifted the yoke from their backs, and it was never to go back on. I will never forget the flags and banners I saw hanging from the small town hall and from the post office as we rode into Gulyai-Polye for the first time:

'War on the palaces, peace to the cottages!'

and:

'On the side of the oppressed against oppressors always! The emancipation of the workers is the affair of the workers

themselves!'

And this hanging from the building that housed the local Soviet:
'**Power generates parasites! Long live anarchy!**'

Now this was closer to my heart, as my head ached from all the
problems I witnessed in the Kremlin. All the handwritten orders
and forms to be filled in, all the desk work and administration
seemed insignificant and somehow underhand when compared
to these brash washing-line banners. Here in the southern
countryside, the revolution was taking hold with the force of an
unstoppable fire. The question of land ownership, which seemed
so problematic when discussed in the drafty offices of the
Kremlin, was being solved in an ongoing day-by-day revolution,
and solved again and again when reality caused bumps along the
way; the livestock, the estates, the factories were to be shared by
all. There were no exclusions. Prisons were outlawed, soldiers
fought for republics of the self held in federation with the arms of
others. This was it!

Mahkno's Anarchy was a contingent democracy, constantly
renewing itself and calling itself into question. In Gulyai-Polye
and surrounding villages peasants' communes had taken over the
day-to-day running and administration of village affairs; post,
communications, housework, childcare, husbandry of the fields,
grain production, shoe-making, education etc. And this was how
he led his men, how what was to become the Mahknovishna
army organised itself on a basis of equality and shared responsi-
bility. The energy, belief and brute strength it must have taken not
only to fight on all fronts but to adhere to the principles of
revolution at the same time was to leave me in awe of this man.
At a time when Trotsky was recruiting ex-Tsarist officers into his
newly formed Red Army, Nestor commanded an initially
voluntary army of peasants and workers who had to fight on all
fronts; against the German occupiers of our country, against the

traditional Ukrainian landowners, and now the White armies that were gathering to destroy the revolution.

September 15, 1918

Radek and his guards saw us off from the station. I waved at him from my seat, Mahkno already buried in a newspaper. I rubbed Grandpa's watch in my hand as the train pulled away and Radek nodded and waved back. Now the train rattles through the night. My companion speaks little, preferring the company of his pipe and the newspaper to my attempts at conversation. What am I doing? What have I given up? The warm embraces of Anna Petrovna for one! Who was this strange peasant? With a rifle on his back and bullet belts strapped across his stocky chest he looked like nothing more than a Cossack, a bloody black hundred!

Sverdlov had made me one of his famous sandwiches. A practical man, he was a good sandwich-maker and we had joked that Jakov didn't make sandwiches but organised them. Despite there being no butter the bread was well stuffed with roasted peppers and salami. I offered half to Mahkno who grunted his acceptance, although muttering something to himself about Kremlin privileges. Sverdlov was so thin I told him I doubted any of these privileges had ever passed his lips.

A few hours later we passed into the Ukraine near Orel, disguised as nationalist officers. Newly painted German signs marked the border. There were no guards, no Germans in sight, just peasants pouring every which way to escape the devil of their choice; landlords, Germans or the Bolshevikii! We shed our uniforms as soon as we got out of town, and now we are on our way to Golyai-Polye with a group of Jewish anarchists who had some bad news for Mahkno. The town has been retaken by German and Ukrainian troops and many of Mahkno's people have been killed.

September 19, 1918
After a week of falling off my horse much to the delight of these people I can now ride well enough, my hand aches and I have a sore arse but at least I can keep up. There are Germans everywhere now, soldiers pouring back from the front to fight for god knows who. Is everything lost for Lenin, has the revolution descended into anarchy?

I am no more than Mahkno's pet Bolshevik, some call me 'red terror' behind my back loudly enough for me to hear, this name being coined more for my danger to horses than any marshal prowess.

Makhno asks my opinion as if Lenin were in my ear, he wants to know if the Bolsheviks will keep their word and allow independent Soviets in the Ukraine after they kick the Germans out. I'm too scared to tell him I have no idea, and that apart from a letter signed by Lenin/Radek with my credentials I have no special method of communication with Moscow. Until we meet up with Bolshevik elements I am alone amongst the anarchists...

When it looked like we were about to see some action Mahkno asked me if I wanted to stay behind, 'for our actions will set the whole region alight with revolution'. When I answered 'I thought that was the point' he clapped me hard between the shoulders, saying that he would be happy to leave me by a train station for any passing Red Guards to pick me up. 'If I am to be Lenin's eyes and ears amongst you anarchists, what good would it be to stay behind?' Nestor laughed, but I knew he was in some way flattered that Lenin had sent me back with him, so he turned his horse and we rode on.

September 24, 1918
Weapons are heavier than you think, like Kaplan's pistol, this rifle is hard to hold up straight for any length of time without

practice. A raid is planned, to retake Gulyai-Polye. Disguised as Varta henchmen we ride towards Dibrivka and Gulyia-Pole with a force of fifty men. Mahkno is in a Tatchanka, a horse drawn buggy in which there is a machine gun. We ride. It is still very hot and humid. SO FAR WE HAVE NOT EXCHANGED GUNFIRE. These anarchists know the forests and the steppes too well and can appear, disappear at will, changing their horses in most villages they come to, they pay for food and forage in cash or promises always fulfilled. Indeed in every village we visit we pick up recruits, boys, men, willing to take up arms against their oppressors. At night we sit round low-burning fires and listen to stories of white armies sacking villages and Cossacks massing on the Don preparing to destroy Soviet power, but by day we seem to travel the lands east of the Dneiper unopposed.

It took two days to reach the town, and we have taken some German prisoners, thanks mainly to our speed and good disguises. Mahkno walked into one hamlet dressed as a woman to make contact with his people there. This is a strange fairytale! Everywhere we go we come across enemy soldiers, but not many of them willing to fight. The end of the war makes these men bad soldiers. Mahkno disarms them and tells them to go home and wrestle their own lands from the grip of the landowners. He rarely kills any prisoner out of hand, but is brutal with any who stubbornly oppose him. Any soldier who has to be disarmed twice is immediately shot.

September 26, 1918 – Outside Gulyai-Pole
Today Mahkno sneaked in and out of town alone to attend meetings. We camp outside the village of Pokrovske twenty miles to the north. It's all set, we wait, will tomorrow be my first taste of fighting?

I recall that night, only remembering it fully as I write it down, and then revising it when the words on the page don't line up with those in my mind. Each word spoken either returns or is lost forever to be replaced by what? Stand-ins, words spoken now, but said then.

Nestor came and sat next to me as I was nervously scribbling in my notebook. He smoked silently, then after a while asked to see what I had written. I think I could have refused him, but for some reason it didn't occur to me to do so. I handed it to him. He read carefully, mouthing the words by firelight. After what seemed like ages he spoke.

'Be careful that your words don't get carried away with themselves Bolsheviki! If I tell you a story and you write it down and then hundreds of miles away somebody reads it even just a few days later it cannot be the same story. Can't you feel it boy? This is a time when stories change. For years they stay the same, and are a comfort, we listen to them like children to their mothers at night-time. But now it's different. Heroes and villains have swapped roles so many times nobody knows what part they are meant to play. Maybe none, maybe it's time to do without them, to do without stories.'

He handed it back to me, banging the bowl of his pipe on his knee.

'You Bolsheviks are like the Whites and all the others, you still need heroes and villains to populate your stories. You need each other. Here, we don't need anybody. The story can be different if you look hard enough.'

I stumbled for an answer to this. 'We all need each other. Doesn't the worker need the peasant, the peasant need the worker?'

Mahkno stuffed his pipe with tobacco and re-lit it, staring me full in the face.

'I'll answer you with another story. When I was your age, we stole 500 roubles from an old man called Kernerenko, a wealthy local nationalist poet. We didn't hurt him, didn't need to, we scared him enough and he could afford it. It was our first successful action, undertaken to fund a printing press and to produce some leaflets. But then a week later a policeman was killed by mistake in another robbery attempt. The policeman was a popular guy in the town and we felt obliged to make amends for our mistake. I was sent to give 100 roubles to his widow and children. I waited until it was dark and crept up to the house. I bent down and left the money folded under a stone, but as I got up the door creaked open and a girl, his widow, stared at me through a crack in the door. She was no more than a girl but his widow nevertheless. I picked the money up from under the stone and handed it to her through the crack. I mumbled an apology. She clasped the money to her breast and closed the door without saying anything, she was shaking with fear of me, probably thinking I had come to finish her off. Within a week we were hunted down and most of my group were killed in a series of shootouts with Tsarist coppers and I was to spend five years in Butyrki prison, a death sentence commuted to hard labour for life. At the age of seventeen. That's my story, but how would it be told in Kharkov, in Kiev, or in Moscow? What is the real truth of this, of these deaths I have recounted? How many sides can a story have, and does each telling replace the truth of the last, or is the truth spilt a little each time so that it becomes empty, just a story?'

I was confused, not to say naive...

'Truth across time and space is what makes us human, how else are we to judge ourselves or be judged by others? The revolution has proved that what you did at seventeen was worthwhile, whoever tells the story, history will judge it to be true.'

'And if it fails, if I fail, then what, who tells that story?'

He got up and left without saying another word. I felt I had disappointed him, and that what was to come later between us was already present in this conversation, foreshadowing the future. As we all know, the winners tell every story, the rest of us stood down as mere facts.

September 27 – Liberation of Gulyai-Polye!
We charged into town and they all ran away chased by fierce peasants wielding pitchforks! These Austrians have no fight in them and now the peasants control the town and have set up a revolutionary committee. Mahkno's presses work overtime printing leaflets explaining what has happened. After a heated discussion at an open meeting it is agreed to send all the Austrian prisoners packing with the news of our victory and the impending victory of revolution in the region.

September 28 – Surrounded!
How our fortunes have changed. Finally I have come under fire, my shoulders sore from hunching down out of way of the bullets, I had no chance to shoot, but I didn't run, we retreated under fire back into the forest! Who was to know we would be back skulking in the forests within 24 hours, hunted on all sides by Germans, Austrians and Varta henchmen. They control the main railway lines and can easily get ahead of us, whichever way we turn. There are rumours of fresh reinforcements from Polohy. We travelled north-east to the village of Velyka Mykhailivka where again the villagers give us food and lodging.

September 30
Last night we were roused from sleep by shouts of an imminent attack and we scattered into the surrounding forest. I lost my rifle, and fear I am not alone in being unarmed. Most of the horses have been captured. In the forest we come upon an anarchist sailor who calls himself Fedor Schuss. He looks more like an eighteenth-century pirate, swathed in furs, with a Tartar hat and long felt boots. He has a band of fifty men and a Lewis machine gun with a few hundred rounds. Some of his men are

badly wounded and he is pessimistic about our chances of escape. There are rumours of enemy troops circling the woods from the rail spur to the north. Mahkno argues with Schuss that 'the only way out of the noose was to kill the hangman' and suggests we attack the garrison of Austrians in the village. Schuss throws his lot in with us. An odd thing, a sailor set adrift on land, somehow sad, somehow dangerous. His men rally and realise they have no choice, 'Or else be hunted down like dogs'. This was what I had come for, to see the poor peasants rise up against their landlords, and throw off the German Imperial yoke into the bargain!

September 31 - Breakout! Battle of Dibrivka.
I live, I live, I live! Our sixty fit men faced about 500 Austrian troops who were camped out in the church square. What odds! Schuss took his Lewis gun and circled to the far north of the town. We enter the town from the south-west, and approach the square. A team of three sets up our old maxim gun by the stable, which has a supply of water to cool it. Crouched by a wall on the south side of the square, I heard Nestor whisper to his men, 'This is it, we are in the arms of death. So friends, let us be dauntless to the point of madness, as our cause demands!'
The Maxim opens fire on the bivouacked men through the rotten planks of the stable wall. Schuss opens up from the other side of the square. Total panic overtakes the soldiers, their officers and the local landowners who had garrisoned the town. The effect of the crossfire was terrible, I saw a man cut in two as we strafed him, the top of his body toppling over before his legs stopped running. The last rounds from both guns gave us our cue to attack. Only adrenalin stopped me from throwing up, as Nestor rose up and led the fight from the front as the enemy were routed through the town. I followed him, I don't know how or why but I felt a great sense of relief

to finally go forward into battle. This was my blooding and it felt good. I screamed and fired my pistol. Did I kill anybody? I don't know, maybe, with all the smoke and noise it's impossible to say. Our peasants chased the fleeing soldiers into the fields and only a gunshot from Nestor prevented them from murdering them. The locals hail Nestor their 'Batko', their big brother. We captured over one-hundred-fifty rifles, another Lewis gun, and two trucks full of ammunition. Nestor executed the Varta members as traitors, and whatever landowners had been captured, but the ordinary soldier we disarmed, fed and sent packing with assurances that they would not take up arms against the people. The village was ours, and the people came out to claim it. So this is revolution, the smell of cordite, the taste of vodka, and a black flag raised in victory over a blood soaked earth. So be it.

The Germans were back two days later, and we were back in the forest heading south. The village was destroyed by an artillery barrage and then set alight. Over six-hundred houses were destroyed, god knows how many people were killed or women raped. That was their revolution. Makhno and especially Schuss were hardened by this. What makes a revolutionary? What allows them to rise above the daily toll of their actions? To exist on a level where life and death are in your daily gift, and your life or death is in the gift of others. This is the definition of war, revolutionary or otherwise.

October 5, 1918
We watched the village burn and immediately our men took their revenge on the rich peasants' houses in Havrylivka, torching them methodically. From horseback we swooped on the undefended town, cheered on by the poorest elements. Schuss whose own home village we had failed to defend was in the darkest of moods and sought to purge himself in the flames

today, again and again lowering himself from his horse and tossing torches into doorways, or lobbing them up onto thatched roofs. Yet neither Mahkno nor Schuss drew their sabres. Now the true meaning of civil anarchy makes itself known. The purgative bitter taste of soot fills the air as I stand outside another burning synagogue.

Another burning synagogue, easy to write, and now with a flourish of revolutionary style, perhaps expressing the arrogance of still being alive, but how quickly I had circled back to this point, this burning synagogue, yet it was true that we burnt as many churches in the months to come.

After a month of defeats, victories, captured trains, released prisoners and burnt villages, Mahkno felt strong enough to retake his home town and finally give his insurgency a permanent base of operations. Again we entered the town without a fight after nationalist forces in the surrounding area had come over to our side. It was only after this first rush of excitement that we were to discover who had been killed in Nestor's absence. Members of the town's first soviets, anarchists, Jews and Nestor's older brother Emilian, who had been shot in front of his wife and kids, a man almost blinded in the Russo-Japanese war fifteen years earlier. Hangings, shootings, children speared on bayonets, rape, pillage and burning had all accompanied the German occupation of Nestor's town.

Who is Nestor Mahkno?
(Excerpt) Filed January 1919/central archives of CHEKA/NKVD
'...A slight man probably in his early thirties. Dresses in the common style of peasants of that area. An anarchist peasant who had the benefit of five years political education in Moscow's Butyrki prison after a series of armed robberies and expropriations resulting in the murder of a local and popular policeman. Released during the revolution he led a carpenters strike against his former employee and local capitalist

bigwig Vladimir Kerner. There's something of a local vendetta here, but not extraordinary given the circumstances. Established a peasant union immediately after release from prison which is very much his power base. He is committed to non-party Soviets, and in this is supported by the majority of the insurgents. He doesn't hide his derision of what he calls 'Moscow's paper revolution', but does not oppose party organs and activists when and if they come into his sphere of influence. His men have been eager to show me how they did things in the Ukraine. He is a fearless military leader who leads from the front in all actions. He will probably die in this fashion if the war continues. At this point it is unclear how many men he can command, the numbers I have seen are in the low hundreds, but I suspect he can draw on many thousands more.

On the Jewish question he was adamant that there was no anti-semitism in his group and that they punished anybody who preached against the Jews. From what I have seen so far this appears true enough. Although I have seen synagogues burn, they are not alone in the flames that ravage the Ukraine at this time. He is against division of any kind. For Mahkno everybody has the opportunity to join with him, to build a new world and reject the beliefs and prejudices of the old. My first impression is that Mahkno and his peasant army are a valuable asset to the revolution and one we can ill afford to antagonise. He will fight the white armies on his land till the very last man, which will probably be himself.'

My time amongst the Mahknovists was not that dissimilar to the story of 'How the west was won', the trail of broken treaties and promises made by successive American Governments to the Native-American population. A childish comparison, inspired no doubt by the cheap cowboy-and-Indian comics we had devoured as kids. It's almost too sentimental to cast Mahkno as a latter-day Geronimo on the one side and the Bolsheviks on the other, but it is strangely apt, or at least as valid as any other description. Nestor at least wouldn't have been surprised that I felt compelled to tell his story in this way, although the question of sides is long past its sell-by date.

The pirate swagger of Fedor Schuss, the tight cut of his crimson cloak, his extravagantly waxed moustaches and gold-embroidered buttons flashing in the dawn light, his fingers burnt from feeding his bloody Maxim gun, were not figments of my imagination. The blood temperature of these people and that of the Soviets was too different, their hearts beat differently, they could never co-exist, their blood could never mingle.

As a boy, as a young man, my confused heart was torn between the two. I had been too close to the fire not to fear it, so was drawn to the cold revolutionary perspective of history, the promises of universal emancipation for the Earth that Lenin was attempting to draw down from the heavens. But who wouldn't be seduced by the passion and wild imagination of Trotsky, my God a Jewish Commissar for War! Like Mahkno, both men biblical in their passions. How could I not succumb to the historical rightness of this *commissar for war*, my mind still vivid with images of Old Testament warmongers and warriors from the stories of our Rebbe that spoke to my soul. That winter it was Nestor's Tarantella that we danced across the Ukraine, plaguing our enemies without remorse.

Amidst the ruins of Gulyai-Polye Nestor comforted his brother's widow, swearing revenge amid the cinders of their burnt-out house. A revolutionary fire was to engulf the peasant population that remained, and Nestor prayed that he could control it. The iron was white-hot, but what substance could be forged from it?

Lenin's grief was quieter, and his revenge infinitely more savage. His older brother Alexander had been hanged in 1887 for an assassination attempt on the Tsar. Lenin had been seventeen, like Mahkno. So it all goes back. Lenin's revenge was no less sweet, no less human for being served cold. A different temperature of blood you see, but the same pain, the same sacrifices. As a boy I thought that this would be enough to reconcile one to the other, but it wasn't. The common ground between the two could not be shared, and I, the token of this doomed relationship, was to be broken in two.

'To everyone, everyone, everyone! The Gulyai-Polye district revolutionary committee announces the seizure of Golyai-Polye by the insurgents: there the power of the soviets has been reestablished. We declare a general insurrection of the workers and peasants against the butchers and stranglers of the Ukrainian revolution, the Austro-Germans and the Hetmans guards.'
N. Mahkno, Telegram, Sept 31 1918.

Friends and Work 1988–1995

'The soup option on the works coffee machine provides a savoury lifeline for the down at heel worker. I remember this very clearly, reconstituted croutons bobbing against my top lip as I scorched my tongue on what was, in effect, a free lunch.'

Anonymous, 'Memories of the workplace', University Press, 1993.

The day I left prison was a monochromatic early-winter kind of day. Everything, including the volume, was muted, the dial turned down low on life. It was as if it had been orchestrated to be low key, another anticlimax in the life of yours truly. A bit like the opening scene in 'Buffalo 66', except I was met by my parents, and I didn't need a piss. There are no gates at an open prison, no razor wire, no heavy doors. In fact you have to look hard to find where the fucking jail ends and the free world begins. Typical.

The drive home was probably the lowest I have ever felt. I had become a kid again being picked up from school by my dad. Somebody said something '…until I got back on my feet…' My sister ignored me. I'd offended her. Why was it always about me? I had ruined much of her childhood, by not being a normal older brother, not being much of a laugh, by being actually, as she got older, a bit of a loser. She was seventeen when I came out of prison and went to Ibiza on holiday with her mates three days later. By the time she came back after a fortnight away I had left home. Baggy house was in, I was out.

After an awkward few days at my mum and dad's I went to London to find my friends. Would four years have changed things too much, were my largely untended friendships beyond repair? Had everyone become grown up with careers, mortgages and kids? Had anyone died? I had kept up with some of them by letter and a few visits, but for at least the last year or so I had turned in on myself, let communication with the outside world slide. Not surprisingly most of them had jobs, especially the girls, except of course the really clever ones who were on the dole or working meaningless temp jobs. I moved into a room in my mate's house in Harlesden, signed on and claimed Housing benefit. There was a boom on and he got me a job on a building site, 150 quid a week, cash in hand.

Harlesden. A real shithole. Half Irish, half black, everybody piss poor, each resentful of the other. Being neither was interesting as you got both sides of the story. If you got pissed in the Irish boozer the Willesden Junction you would hear about lazy black rapists. If you had a cocktail in one of the small shops converted to black wine bars like the 'Pink Pussycat' the jokes were aimed at the drunk, no-self-respect, piss-head Irish. A Mexican standoff pertained between the two communities. We were the invisible third, ghosts that haunted both houses.

This was at least five years before drug-related gun crime and Jamaican 'Yardie' gangsterism brought the area countrywide notoriety. Until then this very British standoff was as quaint to me as the class divide of the traditional English pub, with its public and saloon bars.

We worked for a black guy called Dave London delivering plaster boards to building sites. I didn't feel any withdrawal symptoms from prison life, not at first, I was young enough to throw myself headlong into what I saw as my freedom. For a while £150 a week plus dole and housing benefit, me and my mate Paul were living the high life. Running in boards though was fucking hard work. 'Job and Finish', that was the deal. This could be an easy few hours running boards into bungalows, or a gruelling six hours running them up flights of stairs into flats. 'One man one board' was Dave London's mantra for carrying the really heavy gypsum boards. They came in twos bound together by a strip of glued paper, and tore at your fingers as you separated them coming off the lorry. Plaster boards were easy to damage. If we fucked too many of them Dave would go potty and dock our wages.

There is a true free-for-all anarchism on a building site. Or rather an instinctive disdain for authority and private property, which isn't really the same thing. A glorious laziness, a finely tuned ability to find the easiest route to break times; the papers, a KitKat and a hot cuppa. Or 'Lunch and off' if you were lucky, and straight down the pub. A great two-fingered salute to the world of career advancement, of the stiffs, the suits, the bores and the norms. A workplace in fact where, if you were that way inclined, it would be possible to organise natural working class antipathy to authority into something overtly political. Or that's what I thought and obviously did nothing about.

One time we were working at a Jewish old people's home being built in Pinner. It was quite a posh job and all the bathrooms had expensive gold-plated taps and fittings. These got nicked straight out of the box. The site agent, the gaffer, called the cops in and they questioned all of the workers. None of us had seen anything, we gave them the thousand-yard stare. I probably wasn't the only one there who had been inside. Fuck man, this could have been the thirties, a great working-class slouching insouciance in front of the pigs, an arrogant, 'didn't see nothin' guv' accompanied by a longer than usual drag on the fag, or a quick flick and grind of the butt. The police weren't even that fussed, it was a game for them too. The next day the replacement taps were nicked as well. The site agent went apeshit. Again, nobody had seen nothing. Then all the paint and the window frames went walkies. I mean, I do not understand how anything gets built in this country. It's wonderful. No wonder old people's homes are so bloody expensive. Maybe they shouldn't have gold taps.

Hard physical labour is also fucking tiring. Most afternoons we would almost inevitably fall asleep on the tube home and end up being nudged awake at the end of whichever line we were on. Dog-tired we would struggle with two pints of a night before falling into bed, a wormhole to the alarm clock ringing and the next day's graft. We smelt of hard work, sweat and plaster. Our fingers had daily cuts, bruises and abrasions, which layered themselves on each other, building up over time into works of art self-titled 'Workers' hands'.

On some sites we worked alongside Irish navvies. Real throwbacks to the fifties. Middle-aged guys in cheap suits who dug holes. Who drank, well, threw back is a closer description, three pints of Guinness every lunchtime. Who argued with their wives about money for food. Boiled bacon and potato type of guys. Every night another five or six pints. Men. Guts of steel, constitutions of oxen. Our local was the Willesden Junction Hotel, a great old Victorian boozer where Hurricane Higgins practiced his snooker upstairs in the 1970s. There would be weddings most weekends and weddings meant fighting. Not mean modern knife fights, but great stand-up and knock-down pub brawls. Expressionistic bouts of male violence, nineteenth-century fighting. And we sat there defending our pints of lager from flying bodies, from collapsing towers of manhood crumpling to the floor in front of us, enjoying the spectacle.

'Spade head' collected glasses, an alert weasel of a man, his pallid skin oozing grease, rivulets of black hair snaking down his skull. His head was blunt and square hence his name. Fucker was a sneaky mean fighter, potting brawlers from behind as he made the rounds, gesturing empty glasses and muttering 'Dead. Dead. Dead', without so much as a question mark as he went. This world existed behind a heavy red velvet curtain that hung from the door, an ancient pub full of drinking men and their women, cloaked from the world.

In the year I came out of prison, Harlesden was what I imagined parts of New York must have been like. Places where progress and modernity weren't as obvious as in other places, where *now* was still more like *then*. I am not being overly romantic in saying this, because there was development and progress, but in these pockets of the developed world they were expressive of older and more persistent cycles of life. Progress, projections of the future didn't seem that important. The young Irish women we talked to and sometimes managed to sleep with from the pub were nurses, social workers, temps, secretaries, who had to deal with men as people who drank, whether it be fathers, brothers or boyfriends. They were very modern in their attitude to sex, which was great, but very ancient in their acceptance of booze; 'The drink' was a fact of life.

My only political activity at this time was to buy the *Morning Star* off Monty Goldman outside Finsbury Park tube station. Me, usually covered in plaster and paint, dog tired and the very image of a daily Worker! Monty was the classic London Commie Jew, his dad had fought Mosley down Ridley Road, and we supported him at every election. The *Star* would advertise Seder nights, Jewish dinners, with Klezmer bands and speakers, usually survivors of the Holocaust. In the mid-eighties some of these survivors were still relatively young, just approaching retirement age. An odd compression of time, it felt like to me, that these people now lived in North London. These Jewish nights run by the paper, and by the CPGB, would be held in places like Earlham Grove in the Cypriot community centre. The horror of the century washed up in the suburban corners of a multicultural metropolis.

We'd donate a few quid to the fighting fund to keep the paper afloat and then spend the rest in pubs, getting fucked and smoking Marlboro lights and lurching unsteadily up out of our seats for the last-orders rendition of the Fenian Anthem, chucking coins into buckets for unread copies of *Republican News*.

On our street was a family of tinkers. All fifteen of them. So many boys, young men and teenagers they were a society unto themselves. Everyone called them 'The fucking micks'. They stole anything they could lay their hands on. They were obsessed by cars, as if they had just been invented. The older ones were always working on one vehicle or another, changing a door, beating out a bonnet, lying under the engine, oil pouring out over the road. Their front door was always open and the windows always broken, cardboard invariably taped over the holes. Pieces of broken things littered their front garden and spilt out into the street in front of it. I mean they were a fucking unbelievable cliché come to life. This was another way of life, almost eighteenth-century in its rhythms. Their accent was so thick you understood one word in seven. One of the sons would involuntarily cross himself every time he got into a car, or went through a door, a jerking almost robotic gesture that he had little awareness of and that was invisible to the rest of his family. I became obsessed watching him, counting the times he did it, averting my eye if any of them saw me looking out of the window.

They didn't mix, or play neighbour. They fought amongst themselves and other tinker families in the neighbourhood. In fact there exists a parallel universe of tinker families across, for all I know, the world, where they feud about cars. Coming back from clubs at four in the morning, I would regularly stumble upon a police/Mick stand-off. The cops would cart one of them off for some petty misdemeanour and the others would face off the police brandishing pool cues. The pool cue was their weapon of choice, quaint somehow by comparison with everything else.

This was the life I led when I came out of prison. A London life, in the margins of the city that was in many ways unchanged from the fifties or even earlier. We had been the last generation of people to go to university and not use a computer. These few years in this very old city repaid me my years inside, and gave me back my fight, my bounce, which at 29 deserved to wax a little longer.

Building sites and the men that worked on them, the rituals that circumscribed this work and the physical tiredness that such labour provoked, were what linked the past, present and future of all big cities. The pubs, bars, bookies, whorehouses and football grounds that serviced these men marking a line of continuity. The notion that the image of a man digging a hole was still what most people would recognise as a job of work. Labour had currency and this image was central to the currency of labour; a universal symbol. For me this was all that stood between the modern world and a post-modern nightmare. Long after anybody had ever picked up a spade, a shovel, the memory of it, the signification of it, still communicated. The moment that this image weakened, became contestable, or the kids just didn't get it, then things had really changed. This probably happened in 2003.

Dave London lived in Gospel Oak, on a futuristic housing estate built in the late sixties. A real social experiment sort of place. He would pay us each Friday outside Gospel Oak tube station 'weighing us off' from a roll of crisp fifties in his balloon-size hands. We were young, this was real life. Being 'weighed off' by Dave London was fucking cool. One day he summoned us to his flat. We knew something was up as we had never been there before. On site that week there had been complaints about us sloping off early. Dave sat us down in his kitchen. He looked at Paul with what can only be described as his 'deadeye stare'. He spoke to me whilst staring at Paul. Clever trick that.

'Is he taking the piss?'

How did we know that Dave was talking to me but looking at Paul? No idea, but if you were there it was obvious.

'No mate', I replied, 'Don't be silly, he's a good bloke'.

He said it again, with no discernible change in emphasis.

'Is he taking the piss?'

It was fucking scary, because where do you go with that? It

wasn't a question, he was just measuring our balls. I hadn't noticed that Paul had also trodden dog shit all over this lunatic's carpet, his eyes kept flicking down to it. Neither, thank God, had Dave.

'Fuck off then.'

This broke the silence and we scarpered. Not before noticing a Takana sword hanging on the wall in the hall. A year later, long after we had stopped working for him, we heard that he was banged up for taking the sword to his missus.

By 1989 we were pretty much fed up with manual labour. It was fucking painful and knackered you out, putting you in bed by 10 o'clock max, even at weekends. This was the start of the rave years, E, warehouse parties etc., and we wanted to get laid. It was my chance to engage with the present, do something now, drop out in a contemporary visible way, not in the timeless invisible way of repetitive manual labour. Our last manual job really showed us the writing on the wall.

We got a gig working at a newly completed private sports club in Barnes. I remember it being opened by Annika Rice, then a big-deal TV presenter of 'Challenge Annika' fame. It had indoor tennis courts and swimming pools. I had my very first posh orange juice from the bar there gratis every lunchtime. It was a very now place for 1989 or so. We had laid the fucking floor of the tennis courts without a clue because the site manager had run out of cash and asked us to do it. Looked more like a crazy golf course than a tennis court and I think they had to redo it the week after we left. Our next job was to spray the brickwork of the whole place with a special transparent sealant. This would take about a week. On the first day a bloke drove up in a truck and asked us if we wanted to flog him the tins of sealant. There was a whole shed-load of them and he'd give us three-hundred notes for the lot. The site was in such turmoil, everybody running around trying to get the place finished, it even had the first members turning up for a fucking swim with their kids, that nobody noticed what we were up to. 300 quid. Coke, Es and booze sorted for a few weeks. The problem was we had to finish, or pretend to finish the job. We spent five days spraying water onto the brickwork. Believe me, pretending to do something like that is a lot worse than actually doing it, by a fucking mile. I mean it really did our heads in. I hope that fucking place is crumbling with acid rain corrosion, because we paid for that sealant many times over. So. The end of manual labour. What came next was in many ways worse.

I got a temp job working as a clerk in law offices just off Lincoln Inn Fields. Mindless paperwork, a typical office job. I would also nick the change from the honesty box of the coffee machine. On the third day I was carrying some papers along a corridor when I saw somebody (an idiot) from university. Shit. He spots me and smiles, says hello, what are you doing etc. He assumes that I'm a barrister like him. 'I'm just temping actually', my fingers deep in my bulging pockets making sure the coins didn't jangle. 'Oh that's great, see you around then.' Suffice it to say I didn't go back to work after lunch. Next, a successful friend from college gets me a job in sales. Cold-calling offices selling them coffee and drink dispensers. Well, to be precise, arranging for one of our sales people to go in and demonstrate the machine. This job consisted of a desk, a phone and a copy of the Yellow Pages. There were six of us and when somebody made an appointment it was the convention that they rang a bell on the wall. It signified success and commission. We had lunch in a place called 'Honey for the Bears'. When I couldn't afford to order a sandwich I told the others I had a dentist appointment that lunchtime and sat in the park reading my book. When I could afford to eat, I annoyingly developed the common habit of always ordering the same thing. A sausage sandwich with brown sauce, a cup of tea and a KitKat (cold from the fridge). I looked forward to lunch and daydreamed about what awaited me. Got to be embarrassing when the cafe workers would shout out

'Usual?' every lunchtime. I would nod. Occasionally they ran out of KitKats and I panicked, but would manage to compose myself enough to order a Twix instead. My habitual nature was revealed, making me look all too human and not very cool. Out of spite, mainly to myself it has to be said, I would sometimes spit out 'Spanish omelette and a coffee please'. Heads turned, the waiter gave me a look as if to say 'really?' I nodded. If you had to count that as one of life's victories then you knew you were in trouble.

The job lasted three months. I found I was very good at closing the appointments, yet I couldn't bring myself to ring the bell, which spoilt it for everyone else. I was seen as being too good for them, a clever cunt, who did I think I was, reading at his desk during breaks? On my birthday we went to the pub for a lunchtime drink. The pub had a stripper and somebody told her it was my special day. She came over, took my specs off my face, and whilst dancing slid them between her legs and popped them back on my face. I was thirty-two years old. I could smell the stripper's pussy under my nose. I started to cry which again spoilt everyone else's fun. I walked out and remember leaving my favourite green cardigan on the back of my chair in the office. It had holes and my old Soviet lapel badge depicting missiles on the back of flatbed trucks parading across Red Square under a banner exhorting the Red Army's proficiency with tactical nuclear weapons. I loved that badge, and the musty smell of that cardy, musty from the year at university I spent living in Brightlingsea, in a house profoundly damp with sea spray and rain.

I just couldn't bring myself to ring the bell. God knows where the people that did are now. The only person I spoke to from that place was somebody called Chris from the sound system Rap attack. I wold see them every year at carnival, outside the Tabernacle. He was a good bloke and had no problem ringing the bell, I just hope he got out.

I can still smell the stripper's cunt on my glasses. Not even a particularly cuntish smell, more a cheap soap from the dispenser in the bogs smell underscored with sweat. Smells are persistent and manifest themselves as key parts of memories.

When I was six my dad had the bright idea to send me to a prep school. He wanted the best for me. Nobody in our family had ever been to one etc. He had the money, worked hard for it. So to the dismay of my grandparents and, I assume, my mother, I found myself with a wooden tuckbox, endless pairs of grey flannel shorts, a cool elasticated twisted snake-buckle belt and a grey cloth cap piped in crimson. Hurstpierpoint College. Second-rate prep school. I met very exotic kids whose parents were overseas. I remember one boy called Ashley whose dad was a pilot for Cathay Pacific. My best friend was Richard Skipp who came from Farnham in Surrey and who wanted to work with animals when he grew up. So did I! In ancient Mr White's maths class I would sniff the strap of my dad's watch that he gave me as a going-away present. It was his smell, my dad's. When it grew faint all I had to do was lick it to revive it. It was made of a brown woven fabric and must have stank by the time I was taken out of school after a severe bout of pneumonia that had put me in the sanatorium when I was nine. There was also Mr Clarke who smelt of Old Spice aftershave, our gauche music teacher who liked using the belt, tall kindly Mr. Paul the headmaster, who despite his kindness had a glass case in his study housing two canes. Mrs. Cundy Cooper from Australia, and our English teacher Mrs. Lyons who had had polio as a kid and couldn't smell anything. Finally and most importantly a certain Mr. Howlett who taught art. At seven years old he introduced me to the joys of hex-based wargaming. We would assemble, paint and adapt Macedonian warriors and elephants to the minutest degree of detail, and pit them against Roman or Thracian armies. We built correctly scaled scenario boards out of plaster-of-Paris. With ranged, mellee and cavalry forces, ten die, a rulebook as thick as my thigh, and numerous measuring devices we waged ancient war in the brightly lit art room. Soon we were building exact replica Tamiya models of German forces from WW2. Flak 99 gun emplacements, specific units from 'Das Reich' battalion, Kubelwagens, King Tiger tanks, something werfens. These were mainly defence-orientated scenarios from the Eastern Front. Only in the Ardennes did we play an attacking German force, and that with limited lines of supply. So you see 'it' started then. Was this guy a crypto fascist? Funnily enough he looked like the guy from post-punk electronic band Sparks, who looked like Hitler, but I don't think so. He just had very specific gaming enthusiasms. Also we would watch projected movies every week in the drama hall. I remember the cold nights walking down to the hall and sitting in the dark with some tuck (crisps usually) and watching blockbuster war movies like *Guns of Navarone, Ice Cold in Alex, A Bridge Too Far, The Longest Day, The Railway Children, Tarka the Otter*. But mainly war movies. So you see for a young boy in the early seventies, the war, 'the world at night' as was, wasn't all that long ago. In fact it was ever-present from my early childhood onwards.

Years later Paul and I would find ourselves in a Turkish pub in Dalston playing pool on speed arguing about the deployment of Jagdpanzer in the closing stages of the war, or the political composition of Jewish partisan groups in the Lvov area of the Ukraine and the merits of...

About that time our then-girlfriends would came home from work to find us watching *Blockbuster* on TV, a quiz show where you had to ask the host, Bob, for a letter to start a question. We would sit there smoking fags, not even drunk, shouting out 'P please Bob', or 'C Bob, for CUNT', pissing ourselves laughing and rolling about on the (filthy) carpet. Real catches we were, for sure, something had to change.

One week we had both applied for two jobs each in the media *Guardian*, Paul for the post of researcher at the BBC, god knows what department, and I for post of assistant subeditor of the *Voice* newspaper in Brixton.

Last men standing, 4pm on a cold Wednesday in March, turfed out of the pub, pissed, jagged on speed, crying out of a terrible fear of rejection. In those years I never heard back from a single job application. Signing on was changing, we had been doing it long enough to notice the transition from getting the dole, which was (or could be seen as...) glamorous and prole-tarian, to becoming a recipient of jobseekers' allowance, which wasn't.

The staff became client advisors, so it wasn't fun for them either. The dole office was open-plan. They were hiding the whole them-and-us aspect of it that made being piss poor at least morally palatable. They had ruined the story. Gone were the days of pulling up outside the dole office in my refurbished sports car (another story), hopping out to sign on in a queue of blokes in paint-splattered overalls, or on huge mobile phones doing dodgy deals, insolent in the face of the government clerk, who himself didn't give a fuck and according to his lapel button badge was a fellow traveller if not a member of the Socialist Workers Party. All gone. Times had changed but we hadn't and were funnelled onto endless restart courses and client advisor interviews.

Restart was a business-orientated workshop for the long-term unemployed. We had to go or lose our benefits. So one day I found myself sitting next to some cunt who wanted to discuss his business plan. This consisted of bottling the water from the well he uncovered in his back garden and selling it as local mineral water. Fuck me. Another guy thought he had figured a way to replicate the smooth motion of the Rolex watch's second hand. Really. This knowledge would make him millions in un-spottable fakes. The advisor had to go through with this charade in order to earn her (no doubt paltry) wages, so we were both trapped, both scraping the bottom of the barrel. This at a time of high capitalism, when some of my university friends were well on the way to becoming millionaires. In recruitment consultancy for fuck's sake.

Ring the fucking bell? The bell was tolling all by itself.

Reading, playing pool, drinking, sniffing speed, reading, watching the world go by from this odd distance that I, and not prison, had created. A distance that I felt had become uncrossable. I was there but not there, thoroughly outmanoeuvred and kicking myself for being so stupid. Really up shit creek, and bitter and twisted and paranoid with it. Thatcherism had come and gone, history had come to an end and then started again. But me? What?

So you see I became an Anarchist because I had no other option. I admit it wasn't from any idealistic urge, or from any close reading or study. Like people who do great things for charity, more often than not it's because somebody in their family had leukaemia or whatever. That's the way it goes, until it happens to you who gives a fuck? And boy it was happening to me, I felt I was being squeezed out, erased from the picture like a fucking Trotsky.

So my change in life was born out of necessity. This sense of no other option, which I freely admit was one fostered by my fevered imagination, heated by the constant ringing of tinnitus, was to provide me with a resilience that surprised everybody not least myself. Idealism dilutes itself with every disappointment. But necessity, not seeing any other option, a desperate necessity, was to open many doors and provide me with a wonderful life.

Cheka Mate

'Gentlemen capitalists of Russia and abroad! We know that it is not possible for you to love this establishment. Indeed it is not! The Cheka has been able to counter your intrigue and your machinations as no one else could have done, when you were smothering us, when you had surrounded us with invaders, and when you were organising internal conspiracies and would stop at no crime to wreck our peaceful work.'
Lenin, December 23 1921.

I was tired, tired and numb. Civil war overwhelms the senses and overloads the intellect, it is familiar, ancient, its rules of engagement more akin to patterns of domestic violence than orders of battle. The violence never comes from one direction, it swamps you. An historical violence, a violence of the earth unleashed by seismic shifts in society to which we were both subject and object. Slowly I became distant from it, an astral projection hovering over myself. When not exhausted I questioned the very notion of free will, of my free will, in the things I did. At 23 I should have been a student of life not it's master.

Sunset on the banks of the Dneister, late in the hot and humid July of 1923. I sat on my horse chewing sunflower seeds from a paper cup. Mishka, swished her tail to ward off the flies. Disguised in the irregular costume of the nationalist army, a Circassian sabre in my belt, bandolier of cartridges crossing my chest and a cocked Tartar hat that reminded me of Fedor Schuss. I cut a striking figure, in this last act of our revolutionary war. I was to accompany the returning White General Tutyunnik to a meeting of the (non-existent) supreme Ukrainian military council.

In reality I was production manager and leading antagonist in the threadbare production of 'Capturing the Last White General'. We worked behind the scenes as well as on stage, like a company of poor traveling players under the Tsars. Now it was time to perform. For two months we had infiltrated the White's Romanian village HQ, our agents persuading the General and his staff that Ukraine would rise in support of him, and the time was ripe for one last push against the Reds, that the defeat of the anarchists had left a vacuum they had yet to fill and that he should come home, before the Red Army consolidated its hold on the countryside. Him and what was left of his army, barely a hundred men. The General heard what he wanted to hear, although carefully sending his own emissaries across the river to gauge the mood of the villages. We faked reception committees, held village meetings, brought in actors to play nationalist supporters, peasants and workers, bribed families, held hostages, so that all his emissaries returned back across the Dneister with good news. Finally he agreed to return, persuaded by a fatal mix of inertia and vanity, who knows? But he would only cross the river escorted by the local insurgent commander, namely me, Pyotr Semyonov.

Reluctantly I got down off my horse, feeding her the last of the sunflower seeds. The young ferryman smoked sullenly and urged me to hurry as he didn't want to make the return crossing in the dark. Fuck him, he had made a tidy sum these last months ferrying us players there and back. Darkness had become my friend, in it was where I felt the most comfortable, so I took my time getting into his damn boat.

Night at last. The sun had set and a hellish glow bathed the Banks of the Dneiper. I looked east, away from the last squibs of light. I brought Tutyunnik down into the boat myself, persuading him of the safety of darkness. His heavily armed escort followed.

The crossing of the river Stix was never better staged than on that night, as we sat on the gunwales, exchanging whispered confidences and cigarettes. I offered him my hip flask, a gift from

Mahkno on my twenty-first birthday and now filled with apple brandy. Two-hundred Red Army soldiers waited on the Ukrainian side of the river hidden behind a convenient berm that ran parallel to the river bank. On top of this berm, my fifty Chekists and assorted actors made camp in expectation of their leader and saviour of the Ukrainian people General Yurko Tutyunnik, the murderer of countless Jews and unarmed peasants and now number one enemy of the people. His watery eyes drilled into me. A face he had seen by firelight many times in the last month. He spoke quietly, yet as if from a distance.

'Pyotr, I know you and you know me. We won't fool each other. This is all a fiction isn't it?'

I drank deeply and handed the flask back to him, the burning spirit in my throat commandeering my choice of expression. The boat slid across the river and his eyes held the question. His men adjusted their belts, their sabres and guns. Martial noises of metal on metal, metal on leather, low coughs and the crossing of legs. They hadn't heard him.

He knew yet couldn't resist, hypnotised by the deep whirring of history in the unravelling of that moment. He was armed, his troops on the far bank were as yet unmolested, yet I was safe, invincible even as I held his gaze and replied.

'Oh no sir, it's real, you're coming home.'

We both existed at the same distance from ourselves, from force of habit, from being brutal and being brutalised by war.

He smiled sadly to himself. 'Home is always real, perhaps the only thing that is which is why we fight so desperately for it.'

I nodded agreement to this nonsense.

Tutyunnik and his men were arrested without a single shot being fired. They sleepwalked into captivity, the remaining troops across the river dispersing or crossing in dribs and drabs over the next weeks, uniforms discarded, weapons hidden in barns or under floorboards not to be used for twenty years. Over the next months the General wrote letter after letter denouncing the Ukrainian Nationalist cause as we consolidated our support in both the towns and villages of Galicia and greater Ukraine. When that was done he fell out of a prison window.

But this work had severed me from the very reality I was helping create. To be honest I couldn't take anything very seriously anymore, or in fact took it all too seriously and was immobilised by a general and all-pervading horror. In the lucid moments on waking after sleep, I wanted to cross the river myself, never to be tempted back, to follow Nestor west, cleanse myself in its waters, and escape this waking dream.

Cyber Diaspora

(Or, the Prophesy of the Broken Tiles)

'The miserable decision of the ministry of trade and industry is a badge of shame for the state of Israel. While in the Western world the amount of unnecessary animal experiments is gradually being reduced, Israel is becoming the dumpster of the world. Everything that is forbidden in modern countries is allowed here.'
Nechama Ronen, Knesset member, April 2002.

Homework – My Grandfather

My grandfather was a fascist from Europe. My dad says he was a partisan. My grandmother used to say he was a traitor. I don't really understand these words and I never knew my grandfather. He was Ukrainian. I am an Israeli. Am I also Ukrainian? Or Russian? Who am I? And what's more, do I give a shit?

4/10. And do you? Needs more...

Mum and Dad are from Ukraine, but speak Russian. The Russian I know is either useless fairy-tale phrases read to me by my mother or bitter Cold War words heard from my father. My parents and I literally don't speak the same language. They lived in Kiev. My father had a previous marriage, but his first wife left him. I have a stepbrother and sister I have never met. Discovering his second wife was Jewish was like winning a lottery ticket for my father. Kind of ironic don't you think? Him and my Mum came to Israel as soon as they could get visas in 1982. Adios mother Russia. I was born in Tel Aviv in 1984, a late surprise for my mum who was forty. Dad got a job in an electronics factory. Mother had me and then started work in a hair salon. They didn't have any more kids.

From the age of twelve I had my own key, which I wore round

my neck on a piece of string.

Russia had been fucked over totally by the end of the Cold War. 'At least fucking Cold War kept us warm', my dad used to say in Ukrainian. He could be Ukrainian or Russian, sometimes in the same sentence, as if somehow the language of one inhabited the body of the other. He had worked since his youth at a power station in Kiev. Dad and his friends used to get very drunk in Tel Aviv cafes making jokes about the fucking Jews, how that in the old country they were either Kulaks or Communists, but thank God he married one so he could get out of there. One time he came home with a bloody nose after a punch-up with some proper Jews from Dnepropetrovsk. I would hear all of this, as he dragged his conversation back with him to our flat along with his friends. I hated him for being drunk, but also for being weak and ignorant. Still for him our Jewishness was a winning lottery ticket, the numbers tattooed on the arm of history. I don't think he ever escaped this irony and therefore never could enjoy his new life in any meaningful way.

Nostalgia would cloud his memories of 'home', in the aftermath of its humbling by the West. His brother would spin him terrible yarns over the phone about Ukrainian women whoring for American and English businessmen, of pensioners and veterans queuing for hours in the driving snow for food, of mafia gunfights and crooked building contracts. Of curfews and random violence. This last closed the circle between past and present and they would both fall silent before hanging up, ambulance sirens in both backgrounds offering a surprising moment of stereo for both listeners.

Increasingly my father would succumb to this past, like a man trapped in quicksand, who eventually gives up the struggle to stay afloat and slides under. I would come home to find him slouched over the kitchen table, drunk. He would goad my mother with nasty shit from before either of them were born. How that the ravine of Babi-Yar was full of not just Jews but

Ukrainians too, the mayor himself had toppled into the pit watched from the tree line by his father, my grandfather. My mother's frayed nerves showed in her hands that would spill the vodka she poured them both to drown their separate sorrows. 'The Jews were first', she finally muttered, unused to and uncomfortable with having to identify herself with these old dead Jews, shocked that the cause of their erstwhile good fortune had now crept between them. Like the recurrence of an old illness, their remission from history was over. My relationship with my father reduced to a repetitive and slurred family history lesson, which could as easily have been science fiction.

My grandfather had been, as far as I could make out, an unwitting Fascist. Whatever that means. He had joined the UPA, Ukrainian Nationalist Freedom Fighters, in 1943. 500,000 men women and teenagers fighting both the Russian and the German occupiers of their beloved homeland as well as Poles along their forever disputed borderlands. In the autumn of 1944 80,000 of these Poles found themselves massacred in a series of villages in the disputed area of Volhyn, under the noses of both the retreating German army and the advancing Russian one. All this is disputed for sure and I don't really know the exact details, it's just another example of death-wish nationalism to me, but I remember these place names, figures, this nomenclature and acronym from before my grandmother died. Only now am I trying to piece it all together. My teachers would be proud of me, not to say surprised, I showed so little interest in their classes. Biographically my Grandpa was in this army, at some point. Some, including my grandfather, fought on after the war, and their last engagement against the Soviet army took place on the Hungarian border in 1956, when irregular units calling themselves the UPA attacked Soviet checkpoints in support of the uprising in Budapest.

They were wiped out. Swatted like flies. Like Japanese soldiers hiding on remote pacific islands, these men were obscene remnants, left-overs, the undead of the Great Patriotic War. My father blamed the Communists for this as well. He had seen his father only a handful of times, his mother had turned her back on her own husband as a traitor after the war, and by all accounts these men lived like animals for more than ten years in the marshes and woodlands of western Galicia until finally put out of their misery. That's how Grandma put it anyway. Her husband had been put down like a rabid dog. She lived with us for five years before dying from lung cancer when I was six. She chain smoked Time cigarettes perched on a stool in the kitchen. My father sat silently drinking as Nana cursed his Nazi-loving scumbag traitorous father, through tears of shame which now I understand to be the signs of perjured love. Equally the tears came as she hawked up her increasingly fragile insides as her clock ran down and her Time cigarettes ran out. As soon as she died my father reverted to calling his dad a war hero.

Shamefully the world's antagonism reverberated in our four-room apartment. Here a barely disguised war was taking place between us and him. The domestic civil war of men vs women. I tried to make the peace by suggesting things, a walk, a game of cards, even offered up my homework for comment, but I failed, any temporary ceasefire lasting only as long as it took to twist the top off the next bottle of vodka.

When the first Intifada came to an end, and the Oslo accords were signed in 1993, he would spend hours on the phone to his brother, seeing if things had got better there and maybe we could go back. This was no flourish of optimism for my dad. But in a newly independent Ukraine there was little work and less money. Instead we moved to Jerusalem. Dad got a better job, in another factory. This one made TVs. Mum found a laundry firm near where we lived, where she did the books as well. It was owned by an Arab guy who had sixteen launderettes spread across the city. One of her jobs was to collect the coins from the machines in the Jewish parts of the town. He was boycotting them. Her weekly challenge was finding banks willing to take all that change. They hated my mum with her bags of jangling coins, this latter-day moneychanger.

She was a good mother. She cooked, sewed dresses, took me swimming, did my hair up nicely, and read to me sparingly in what little Yiddish she could remember. She read me Russian stories filled with snow, a winter wonderland type of snow, full of ice skating children and sleighs and hot mugs of chocolate sprinkled with cinnamon. She was ten years younger than my dad, had been a beautician, her father a railway engineer who fled east with the Soviet Army in 1941. It was his family, his brother and sister, who went into the pits at Babi-Yar. In fact she grew up in her uncle's house, something I only learnt many years later.

My teenage Israel was different, although now I can hardly credit the way I felt. The sun, the sea, the bustling shade and noise of the souk, the modern apartment blocks, the camels, so far removed from my parents' dark and dismal Europe. If I ever dreamt of death, it always came in the snow and the cold, crunching its way towards me.

Apart from her marriage, my mother loved her new life, never questioned it. She didn't become religious at all and was not I think a great Zionist. She always said she liked the look of Shimon Peres on the telly, he reminded her of her Papa, who had died of a heart attack aged 80 watching Dynamo Kiev win the 1990 USSR Cup. She even made some friends, other mothers she met at the kindergarten when I was little. They would go out for dinner, to the cinema or visit each other and play cards and complain about their husbands. Me? I just grew up in fits and starts, periods of sublime happiness followed by passages of failing confidence and self-loathing. By fourteen these forces were in uneasy balance, a truce fraught with risk. In fact from my first period onwards I felt part of the wider world for the first time, a little bit of me felt like a teenager of the world! Music, fashion, boys, cinema, gossip. My best friend Rivka-la and I would pour over the latest magazines sitting in the park, cutting out our idols to paste onto our school folders. She was very serious and dark, also sporty, her skinny neck already cording with muscle as she applied Pritt-stick to the cover of her maths book. I can see now that all this daily life was underscored by a constant low-grade fear, a pressure behind my skull of something terrible about to happen, and when it didn't happen the feeling that it should have, was still going to, and that the delay, unbearable in itself, would only make it worse. Growing up between the wars, between the two Intifadas, was like this. In 1999 I saw the movie *Final Destination* and this was totally how I felt; a creeping dread, a foreknowledge of certain doom. I think doctors, shrinks, call it free-floating anxiety. No wonder the film was so popular, they went on to make many sequels.

We lived in a new apartment block in Gilo, a new suburb right on the edge of Jerusalem. Our flat overlooked a hillside terraced with groves of olives, apricots and vines. Gilo was a housing project for immigrants. Mean concrete lines carving out roads, car parks, shopping streets, unconvincing plots of grass and trees decorating the intersections of this brash layout. It was very functional and decidedly postmodern. I remember the new paving tiles outside our apartment entrance, and how it took only a few months for them to start developing cracks and coming up, so that we would catch the toes of our trainers on them on the way to school. In a place like Gilo you notice these breakages and the discolouration of concrete with sadness and as a harbinger of some future disaster. In Jerusalem proper, a stone's throw north, the crumbling buildings and broken slates, the smelly sewers and discarded ancient building stones are proof of the city's longevity. Here it was the opposite. Our suburb was decidedly rootless, the land itself annexed from the neighbouring Palestinian town of Beit Jalla after the Six-Day War in 1967. Only us children could call this place home, the grown-ups were all from elsewhere, yet when the season of war came round again it was us children who wanted to flee, the others had nowhere else to go.

An old man rode past us on an old creaky bicycle. He was clutching a bouquet of flowers, the stems crushed against the handlebars. Something was interfering with the smooth running of the bike, you could hear the resistance of metal or rubber. He was struggling to get along even though the ground was flat. I felt an urge to call out and stop him, have a look at the wheel, the chain, whatever, anything to make his passage easier. But I didn't call out, I suppose you never do. I wondered where this old man was going with his bunch of flowers. Even though I never saw him again I imagined him doing this journey all the time, that it was his destiny to ride this bike with a bunch of flowers, that he wasn't going anywhere, he was already there. That he was from elsewhere, the flowers, the bike had all existed in another place at a different time in a better condition. The exertion on his old face was something he wanted to bear, because it reminded him of this other place. It was his everyday crucifixion. I think this way about being an immigrant. Your parents want to say nice things about where they call home, but also have to admit why they left. So they are schizophrenic about it. One minute they hated Russia, the next it was the best. One minute Israel is wonderful, the next they want to go home. I find myself avoiding any strong identity. I don't want their passive-aggressive selfhood. In fact having no real sense of belonging is a very healthy personality trait growing up where I did. I see it for the honey trap it is. A homeland, this is your earth, the sky is ours, our birth right. Isn't this just so much bullshit? Everything changes, especially here. Look at Russia, Ukraine, what happened to my grandfather. The land owned him, wed him without pleasure and slaved him to it until death. It was never his land, the earth devoured him. I wanted my freedom from this nationalistic shit because it was screwing everything up. I suppose this is why I spent so much time playing computer games. Towards the end of the century I developed a morbid sensibility that to the outside world was called goth/punk.

I wore dark clothes, blacks and purples. White make-up with smudged Panda eyes. I had a pair of army boots with 18 eyeholes. Some of the boys I knew had camp tattoos on their arms, numbers of the dead, not the survived. I even wore a crucifix. (Upside down of course!) But inside, the feelings of doom and imminent disaster fractured my sense of self-worth. I read in *American Psycho* a scene where the Psycho character finds a dead tramp and puts a lit cigarette in his mouth. Outside our apartment block I put a lit cigarette into the mouth of a sleeping homeless Arab we called Yasser. He woke up choking his guts out. We sniggered from the street corner. How cool was that? Each aspect of my life felt disassociated from the other. Nothing belonged together. Later this would prove my greatest strength. With the effortless power of a Tantric guru I could hold myself apart, literally on the threshold of forming a cohesive whole.

We read about millennial cults, who exult in the coming of the last judgement. Instead of hiding their crazy ideas away they become their public token, they became known for them. That was pretty cool. The bare-faced challenge of it. We sat and awaited the end of the world listening to Marilyn Manson's album *Remix and Repent*. Rivka-la said this had nothing to do with religion. The end was final, uncoloured by belief, just an endless void.

1999

New Year's Eve in Jerusalem was a blast. We took some Es and decided to go up on the Mount of Olives, mingling with the thousands of Christians who were waiting for the second coming. The access roads were at a standstill with traffic. Many were gathered by a modern church called Dominus Flevit. The Lord wept, well it was mostly Americans and Italians. Crying their eyes out hysterically. Fat men, nuns and women with bad haircuts, and lots of overtired bewildered-looking children. These were our tourists. The overwrought.

And all of us surrounded by ancient cypress and olive trees that rustled in the strong wind. It was crazy. Everything in soft mono-colour as sunset fell, we bathed in a flickering golden glow from the dome of the nearby Omar Mosque, and nearer still from the seven domes of a Russian church. Up on Har Meggiddo they waited for the end of the world. The E rolled in and amplified these sounds and colours, the dark storm clouds, the ever present police sirens in the background. This is the place of Armaggedon, so its vibes were pretty freaky, you couldn't help but tune in to them. Literally tens of thousands of Jews and Muslims buried under our feet, the whole hill a cemetery. A sweaty man was shouting himself hoarse, out of both conviction and a need to be heard over the competing trees and sirens:

'And Jesus said to them: "Watch out that no one deceives you. Many will come in my name, claiming, 'I am he', and will deceive many. When you hear of wars and rumours of wars, do not be alarmed. Such things must happen, but the end is still to come. Nation will rise against nation, and kingdom against kingdom. There will be earthquakes in various places, and famines. These are the beginning of birth pains... How dreadful it will be in those days for pregnant women and nursing mothers!"'

And under our breaths we chanted: 'The time has come it is quite clear, Our Antichrist is almost here, It is done.'

The chorus from one of our favourite songs, 'Antichrist Superstar'.

An ancient Shofar sounds up somewhere in the old city, heralding ultra-orthodox curses against the Christ worshippers on the hill. The same curses that had struck down Yitzak Rabin five years before. The ecstasy rode this berzerk noise, that came in waves, three compressed notes oscillating in the millennial wind, a sound obscenely old yet perfect for our mood, we hung on for dear life.

We took our places in front of the famous Golden Gate, the Sh'ar Harahamim, through which Christ was supposed to appear for the second or the first time, depending. This huge city gate was bricked up by Muslims in 810 to prevent the entry of the Jews' messiah, their name for the two arched gates is mercy and repentance, so they must have been expecting somebody. All around are the dead of every faith, the closer you got to the gate the closer you got to someplace special. The City municipality discussed opening it up, allowing Jews easier access into East Jerusalem, which would be sure to anger the Palestinians, but also Christians who were expecting Jesus Christ to be the next person through it, not any old Jewish settler. There was even a fucking live-feed web-cam pointing at it from a parked truck. Christians had no sense of occasion, the ancient vibe dampened by the image of thousands of middle-Americans munching their way through the second coming from the safety of their sofas. We sat staring at the gate, passing a bottle of vodka back and forth. Arab teenagers darted about selling melons and cokes, there was an odd party atmosphere. The E surged, faces started to rouse themselves, primed for the impending confrontation between good and evil as midnight approached. Longer noses, prominent eyebrows, hollow cheeks, wet tongues. Judgement. Throwing down and lifting up. If it was going to happen it would be here and I wanted to be stoned when it all kicked off.

'Prick your finger it is done, The moon has now eclipsed the sun, The angel has spread its wings, the time has come for bitter things...'

What we got was an amazing display of fireworks that broke over the city reminding me of nothing more than the opening credits of *The Wonderful World of Disney*. This made me laugh so hard I threw up a falafel. Christians sang, clapped and chanted until dawn, but to no avail, it was a no show, there was going to be no encore, but by then we had fled the garden of Gethsemane, to a club, a bar, then an apartment. To drink, to smoke, to fuck, to sing, to dance, to keep the gate shut for another few hours, another few days and hopefully, who knew, even years, of our precious youth, times of some little mercy and zero repentance.

In September of that year, Ariel Sharon started the second Intifada proving yet again that you can't go anywhere in this country without treading on somebody's toes. I was sweet sixteen.

Luckily by then I had read a lot and had figured out how to solve the Arab-Israeli conflict. Thank God for me. On the crowded bus to school I worked hard on my solution, as if I was working against the clock. Because in Israel a bus journey is in itself an education and a testament of faith in one's own immortality. Fuck it I was sixteen, I wasn't going to die just yet. Not on this bus.

The Second Millennium
'When you were one you became two. When you are two what will you do?'

I met my first suicide bomber in cyberspace. He told me he lived in Ramallah and wanted to be a politician. I told him that all politicians were scumbags, and that he should look at anarchist ideas regarding the organisation of society. He spat back that kibbutzes had started out as anarchist paradises, now look at them. He supported Hamas, and said that only rich Jews could afford such crazy godless ideas. I said I wasn't rich and didn't feel particularly Jewish. He didn't say anything. I said that kibbutzes couldn't have been properly anarchist because they stole land and didn't share it in common. That gave him pause, I think, which I exploited to send him some web links to look at about animal rights, cosmetic testing and for some reason a Bedouin women's support group site (I don't know why, this last, probably a little patronising on my behalf) that I had just been browsing. He told me that it didn't matter anyway because he would probably be called on to martyr himself in the near future. Although I thought he was lying, I said it would be sad if he did this, for him, his mum and dad and for the people on the bus or in the cafe that he would kill. He told me his father was also an atheist, a supporter of the PFLP, and that he had disappointed his dad. But that his people didn't have guns or planes or tanks, all they had was themselves. I said that killing himself was to admit defeat, was depleting his own side's forces, in fact every suicide was in fact the incremental suicide of the Palestinian people. He was in effect a deserter, doing the IDF's job for them. He disagreed. Asked me why my buddy icon looked like an emaciated Arab girl. His was just a Hamas green flag, not very original I told him, and that the girl was a Kurd not an Arab, called Suriya, who had died on hunger strike in protest at the Turkish government's attempts to eradicate the Kurdish language from the school curriculum. Again the spell of Culture and Homeland, a powerfully unforgiving magic. I asked him to mention her name in his prayers. He said he would. He asked me why Israel was allowed to have nuclear weapons but Arab countries weren't. I didn't know. I hated all weapons, especially nuclear ones. We both blamed the Americans. I told him about the laboratories near Jerusalem where they tested stuff out on monkeys and rabbits. Maybe he could blow that up for me? He blanked this and asked me my name, and I asked his. I read longlivebargouti. He read BuffTatiana. At this point he realised I might be a girl. He logged off, his avatar blinking out leaving me typing into space.

My first actual demo was outside a monkey breeding farm in Haifa. The place breeds Macaque monkeys for export to European testing laboratories, and now to other laboratories inside Israel. These places have started to spread over our country. This was because Israel had signed an agreement with the European Union to conduct animal testing for them because our laws weren't as strict as theirs. The crazy bad karma of this was too much. We skipped school. We got there by bus. There were only about 50 protestors. The police thought we were crazy, but for them it was at least a distraction. They hassled the two Palestinian brothers wearing animal liberation T shirts and Metallica baseball caps. But without relish, this was sideshow stuff. Cars came and went and we shouted at them. It was pretty boring and apart from being there we achieved nothing. A week later a bomb exploded outside the gates of the farm, injuring nobody but destroying a surveillance hut/scaffolding tower, which was pretty cool. Online, we couldn't figure out who had done it, sadly it wasn't us. The next time we demonstrated there, there were lots more of everyone, cops, protestors and an armoured vehicle. We had been upgraded. The Palestinian brothers stayed away, they would have got the blame for the bombing and didn't need the extra hassle. We agreed with them. These were two boys from Beit Jalla, Christians who attended the Taliha Kuun School just off road 60 across from my apartment. A road forbidden now to most Palestinians. These boys had set up the first Palestinian bird-ringing programme there, to track the migration of shrikes and plovers. A week later the authorities arrested an old Jewish anarchist on his fucking kibbutz. It was all over the front page of Haa'retz. We had never heard of him. He got the explosives from his grandson who was doing national service. There were obviously other people out there who felt like I did. The next few years were taken up with finding them and learning about the stuff they believed in. The internet made it easy, and the intifada, this strange civil war in Israel, dragged these inchoate ideas kicking and screaming to life. The West Bank was to be my political education. Water and land and might and control of information were revealed to me as what my world was all about. Everything else was just so much biography.

Walls
Outside our flats the army built a wall to protect us from sniper

fire. We lived on the perimeter of the Gilo suburb/settlement, where the newest and poorest of immigrants are housed. It had the best and most dangerous of views but was in sniper range. The wall replaced the view across the valley. We painted the view back onto the wall, but behind the wall the view changed. Random shots reigned on our building at night. In the morning we would find little mounds of concrete dust, which tiny dust devils threw up into the air, with larger flakes of cement and paint stripped from the walls littering the street. Little kids collected the flattened bullets, traded them for the other shit they collected. The prophesy of the broken tiles was coming true. A year later the army came back and bullet-proofed the outside wall of our apartment block.

Electricity

The town of Jayyous is home to about three-thousand Palestinians, mostly farmers. It is surrounded by Jewish settlements. Jayyous is not connected to the Israeli grid, so electricity is run sporadically from a very expensive generator. Internet access is slow and intermittent because of the continual power outages and self-imposed power cuts. Mobile phone coverage is limited as is the ability to charge batteries for mobile phones.

Land

Jayyous lost 20% of its land to the new Israeli state in 1949, which has since been farmed by settlers. Some of the olive trees of this land are fifteen-hundred years old. The locals call them Roman trees. Old men show me the tattered remnants of Ottoman ownership deeds for this now Israeli-owned land. Now 70% of their land is on the Jewish side of the 'fence'. The fence is a 26-foot-high wall and it snakes across, coils around villages, divides, splits and separates fields and settlements in order to protect Israel and Israeli settlers from attack. Palestinians have to pass through military-controlled gates to work their land. Access is not guaranteed and is in reality an arbitrary privilege ceded by the Israeli army on any given day, or even at the whim of the contractors working on the wall itself. Often they leave huge boulders just inside the gate making it impossible for cars/trucks and tractors to pass through. These gates exist all along the wall separating Palestinian farmers from their land. I have seen Palestinian farmers work their fields by hand alone, like they did back in the day. They go home at night past the boulders blocking the gates, those very hands bloody and ragged, smearing their IDs with shaking fingers. On my unborn children's life, God forbid I should bring any into this world, I testify to seeing this. Anarchists, foreign and Israeli activists of all political persuasions, have set up 'Gate Watch' to monitor this access, that the Israeli government claim is unhindered. Farmers grow olives, apricots, guava, prickly pear and figs. The land that is spring fed is on the 'other' side of the wall. It is prize land. One farmer Abu-Ali had a gun barrel pressed into his head by an 18-year-old recruit as he tried to work his land on the other side. His daughter didn't speak for a month after seeing this happen. She was seven. An old man told me how he used to cross the green line at night to pick apricots from his family's orchard. If caught he would have been shot on sight. He joked that he and his donkey were the apricot liberation front.

Water

I discovered this is what the war is all about, and that water will determine the outcome of this war, and probably many others. Apparently Palestinians and Israelis have different thirsts. Under the Oslo accords Palestinians were granted the right to 57 cubic metres of water per person a year and Israelis 246. Israel has not allowed any substantial Palestinian drilling for water in the 40 years it's controlled the West Bank and demands total control of its water aquifers in any hand-over agreement in return for a joint US-funded project to desalinate water near Ceaserea and pump it back to the Palestinian territory. The cost of this will be at least $1 per litre, way too expensive for any viable Palestinian population, and besides the pipes and control of the plant would remain in Israeli hands. Knowledge is power, but who knows this? Israel also imports drinking water from Turkey by boat. Four fifths of all water in the West Bank was allocated to Israel under the Oslo accords. If the plans go ahead then Palestine will rely more on desalinated water than any country in the world. A desalinisation plant whose pipes run from Ceasarea through the security wall to the city of Jenin. Yet despite this war of water Palestinian and Israeli water engineers have been constantly cooperating and repairing each other's supply pipes throughout war and intifada. An unspoken communality of thirst.

In Jayyous, lands confiscated in 1948 and now on the Israeli side of the green line are now sown with cotton which is the most water thirsty of crops. Jewish settlers get a good price for this premium crop. On the Palestinian side of the green line their water access is controlled by a meter which only allows them to draw a certain amount every month. The Palestinians who operate these pumps are targeted by the Israeli military for harassment, often arrested on jumped-up charges, held for a few days then released. Slowly wearing the men down, slowly but surely stoking the fires of hatred. Regularly Israeli soldiers will shoot out the water tanks on Palestinian rooftops. Hot tanks are prized as targets because they are more expensive to replace, and also might scald those inside.

Settlements

The Israeli settlements are designed to suck the life out of their Palestinian counterparts. Jayyous has a population of 3000. Ariel is 25000 strong. Their irrigated land is protected by the army. Creating facts on the ground that can then be used in any future settlement. Always already making the very contours of the land tell the story. And this is what power can do, it changes historical fact in front of your eyes. The Israelis by resetting the clock to biblical times make it impossible for us to turn back the clock a few years let alone to 1948, to make things right. This is what I learnt. The power of the clock, the power to move those hands at will, to pull the sword from the stony ground, and make it impossible for anybody else to put back. It is now widely considered politically unfeasable to consider the pre-1948 borders, yet it is not unfeasable to look at the Old Testament for legal confirmation of Israeli land and water rights in the twenty-first century.

Movement

Caterpillar bulldozers are used to create roadblocks. These pop up like fungus all along the new fault lines between Israeli and Palestinian land. They are like valves that control movement and hamper daily life on a continual basis, until the wall is completed. It's a cross between Pac Man and Sim City. An underground railroad has been set up to combat these obstructions, to ferry people and goods between settlements and Egypt. A deadly game of cat and mouse. There is a peace camp at the village of Mas'ha, 5 kilometres east of the green line. Here people from all over the world gathered to protest at the building of the wall. As Israelis we were the most valued because we couldn't be deported like most of the foreigners or shot and intimidated like the Palestinians. Also we look good on TV. We were one of them, yet against them. We had rights so we took on the most risky of jobs. The wall was to run east of the village, just past the last house. But this house was also constrained on its left by the fence of the neighbouring settlement Elkana. The house was in effect to be made unliveable in, it had been superceded by history. The peace campers planned a protest at the site for the projected path of the wall that would in effect erase this family from their birth right.

Here I go again, no this is equally wrong, birth right should never be land, but freedom. All this land fetishism is wrong! But when confronted with so much land hunger and obsession with ownership you fight fire with fire and become like them, so it's like we have each other in a death fuck embrace. Total tragedy!

Soldiers came and arrested everyone, firstly the photographers, then the rest. The area had been designated a closed military area and a bulldozer raised the outhouse to the ground to make way for the wall whilst the settlers watched from their hill. We shouted abuse at them, but they probably didn't understand because they are mostly Russian immigrants and speak no English or Hebrew or god forbid Arabic. The only Russian insults I knew were from my grandmother, so I screamed 'Fascist dogs', 'Enemies of the people', 'Kulaks', really outdated stuff that probably confused them, if they weren't confused enough already; the Ministry of Absorption places them in these settlements, throws them to the wolves of history yet again. My face burned with shame and pity for these Russian Jews even as I insulted them, their first day in the Promised Land.

And then we all started throwing stones at each other.

Power

You cannot shame Israel into submission. We are shameless. The wall reminds you of other charnel house walls, so what, you think we don't know this? I read somewhere the ghetto walls of Cracow were crenelated and designed after a 'Jewish style' by the local governor. Power erases the leverage of shame. For the powerless opposition it's all we have. The checkpoints remind us of other checkpoints, the callow faces of too-young soldiers remind us of other callow-faced soldiers. Guns to heads, humiliated men chin-down, laughing soldiers. Shuffling prisoners. The Holocaust is all around us, permeating everything. We ape it. If you teach us about it in school, how can we then not see it on TV? A Palestinian man crosses into Israel for a violin lesson. The soldiers don't believe him and force him to prove it by playing a song. The photograph of the Palestinian playing his violin for an audience of abusive Israeli soldiers makes the front page of the newspapers. Thank god it does, all cannot be lost! His violin teacher is a survivor of Treblinka. Yet we cannot be shamed, for shame doesn't exist for us. I learnt more about the Holocaust from my experiences in the West Bank than I did at school. Force-fed visits to museums and history lessons were boring. Who were these skeleton people being herded about wearing pyjamas? We sloped off for cigarettes. Israel was itself a morality play, an atrocity exhibition of the Holocaust more than any biblical promise, indeed a profane and secular wounding of that very promise.

There is no split between us and them, we are the same story. I am both, and also other, Russian and/or Ukrainian, with my own humours to discover, blood things that pull me, moods and memories that tug my heart and make me wonder. And it can overwhelm, it is too much to carry. I didn't do anything wrong, I hate this burden, so I find myself with my friends seeking oblivion in Tel Aviv's bars and night clubs. Weekends on the beach, paid for with sex and drugs. The clubs were free spaces, outside or perhaps radically inside the law. Places of sensuality, hedonism, with guest DJs from Europe, even from Ibiza. We danced with gay friends, learnt from them how to have a good time. Arab trannies, Jewish dealers, soldiers too. To let go, to feel the beats, the rhythm coursing through your body, to enjoy the blood rush, to discover the galaxy of yourself amongst others. To fuck a lot, to sweat all over another person, to suck them, to be touched and sucked, to experience the cold sweats of comedown, coke shivers and aching teeth, all this is to plunge into a sensual world that is in essence anti-historical, my body's perimeter contained, slaved to the ever-present. How far we have come from the feral hoarding of crusts of bread and sucking rainwater from torn scraps of clothing carefully prodded through the broken slats of cattle wagons, now we drink coffee and chew croissants in beachfront cafes at dawn, our clits and cocks tingling from drug-enhanced pleasures, how much fucking I ask myself went on in the camps, how much pleasure was there to be had in those places and did they take it? Why I think all these things I don't know, but they do come into my head, parsed in Hebrew, a brash modern street-Hebrew but still the language of my inheritance.

2003/Warcraft

One of our friends died IRL (in real life). She was female, I never knew that before she died, her boyfriend contacted us. She lived in Helsinki and was killed when the car she was in collided with a snow plough. Snow, I hated it! Where was she going? Was she driving? How old was she? Who else died? It happened on a motorway at night. Where do motorways go to in Norway, what are the names of the cities they connect? She was a level 57 Mage called Loki who had been a member of our guild for three years. We held a memorial service for her online, in front of a lake by the gates of Amon Rath, near to his birth keep of Vanguul. This was an open game play area, in case other gamers who had blogged her death wanted to attend. As a Guild we were weakened, for she had carried all our herbs, potions and battle spells.

The boyfriend gave us limited access to her passcodes, so that we could have her avatar present at the ceremony. He was planning on taking over her stats and achievements but with a new skin and sadly for us new guild affiliations. There were approximately eighty of us. Some were angry because our loss came just before the new realm of Asteroth was to open and we had planned and trained in the hope of being amongst the first inside. Some of the others suspected the boyfriend had already sold our cache of potions and accumulated skills. When we accessed her avatar her attribute and possession files were already empty, hmm.

The memorial went ahead as scheduled. We uploaded some sombre gothic organ music. By coincidence it was snowing, thanks to the random weather-generating calculus of the game engine. A number of other gamers attended keeping to the tree-line overlooking the gate, leaving the lake side for members of the Guild out of respect. We recognised amongst them allies and trading partners. There was even a group of hill trolls who had turned up to pay their respects, who we had bettered the year before in open Mage-led conflict.

Nobody expected what happened next. Marauders, a raiding party from a rival guild swept out of the ravine that split the hills behind us. We had posted the funeral on an open message board. We had been stupid. Our weapons were piled in honour of Loki by a burning fire. Her avatar was to be placed on top. We dressed it in her finest dress, the green one shot through with gold filaments we had plundered from Marsh dwellers way back on level 46. The enemy guild Sam9 destroyed 80% of our members. They were maxed out on stats, we were fucked. We were all on our knees, in front of the funeral bier when they attacked from three sides. I escaped by diving into the fire and activating my fire protection ward spell, clicking it again and again as the massacre continued by the lake. Flame pixels obscured the slaughter. When I came out my comrades lay about me, Loki's body had been violated and all our weapons, spells gold and property stolen. They had totally bombed us out.

I logged off for the last time.

In country

The night before the hunt we stayed in a grotty little B and B outside Annick. Damp, creaky stairs and floorboards and Cassy stunk the room out with her hairspray. The room made her look a bit grubby to be honest. I felt bad licking her out, a little queasy. I thought of a story a mate told me, the night he got off with this Goth he met at the Marquee. They were so pissed he blacked out and woke up the next morning in bed next to her. He looks up and she's sitting there Jacking up. He rubs his eyes, can't believe it, she smiles offering him the syringe straight from her arm. I felt a bit like that in bed with Cassy, licking her out.

As soon as she came she started talking. I lay there getting my breath back, breathing in all the fucking damp coming off the North Poxy Sea. The gist of it all was that it was pretty hard up north, her dad was a miner and she had grown up in fear of him. She remembered one morning he put his head in the gas oven, the whole kitchen stank of gas and he held up an unlit match in one hand threatening to finish them all off.

'He were a right bastard', she said, smoking the inevitable cigarette.

God she loved fags, 'tabs' as she called them. Economy-brand fags like Red Band, or JPS Super Kings, which were too long in the mouth for the first ten puffs and made you look odd, out of proportion. When she was really skint she smoked roll-ups. Her first and second fingers streaked with yellow with tobacco stains, like old people had. I bought her a rolling machine like my grandfather used. As a kid I loved watching him stuffing it with tobacco, licking the leading edge of the Rizla paper and lining it up with the rollers. It was simple art, a ritual that punctuated every day. I loved seeing the perfect rollie come out of that machine, a bit like working-class sushi.

I thought that Cassy's dad was a self-indulgent loser, and his threats of family annihilation the signs of a weakling. From then on I would notice reports in the papers of similar incidents where men and occasionally women kill themselves and their kids after a marital bust up that conjured an image of Cassy's dad with his big miner's muscles and his head stuck in the oven threatening his child with a match. What the fuck have we done to ourselves that the horror is so readily at hand.

I kept my thoughts to myself, a rare moment of tact, and probably just exhaled a whispered sympathetic 'Christ!' and let her continue talking. Her dad didn't hate blacks because they had one down the mine and it's hard to hate somebody whose back you scrub in the showers after a shift. I didn't realise that miners touched each other in the showers, huh. All these years later I remember what she said but nothing of the sex. This seems to be a rule. Sex is forgettable, it literally dies the moment it comes. That's probably why we have to do it all the time, constantly renew our memory of it, only to have that memory erased as soon as we've experienced it. Sex is a workable definition of habit, and the comfort we seek in repetition. Which is by all accounts a recipe for shit sex. Cassy and her need to talk about her abusive fag father was a real turn-off. Sucking her pussy all I could taste was stale cigarettes, which had to be psychological unless she was stashing them inside herself, which she wasn't, so it was definitely time to move on.

Did I have a problem with working-class women in the flesh as it were? Did I have similar issues with middle-class women, or was it women in general I had a problem with? How could I have this physical response and at the same time believe in all the things I did? Or did I really believe in anything all? If not, what the fuck was my problem?

What is the nature of belief? What is its substance? What does it mean to hold a belief? Martyrs, Protestants like Cranmer Latimer and Ridley, were burnt at the stake for their beliefs. Buddhist monks set themselves on fire for theirs. What is that all about? These people chose to be burnt alive. They held beliefs that were stronger than the hard-wired human will to survive. What they believed was bigger than who they were. Thomas More in *A Man for All Seasons*, all he had to do was sign something, agree with his king about succession, but he didn't on principle and died for the privilege, all the time being begged to recant, change his mind, by his wife and kids. On one level a really a selfish guy; a man and his beliefs, God save us from them. But on the other hand, these people were free, free above all from the physical demands of self.

The next morning I woke up to the smell of her hairspray on the pillow and stale fags. She straddled me half asleep and pushed her too-wet cunt down on my cock. After we fucked and showered we had breakfast and headed off for the village where the hunt was meeting at ten-thirty. On the way sitting at the back of the bus like school kids she talked some more about her childhood. I stared out of the window, half listening, the landscape outside distracting me as it flickered past.

In Northumberland you still get a good sense of the lie of the land as it has been since the Dark Ages. The brutal and sometimes bloody husbandry of fields and forest. A continually contested landscape. Chiefs, raiders, warlords, kings, knights, barons, landowners and developers. The locals were all about this in their relations with each other. Serf/Master/Local/ Outsider. I dozed, daydreaming myself as a ninth-century money-lending Jew, travelling by carriage between towns and castles lending money to drink-crazed Anglo-Saxon lords who lust after my daughter, Ruth/Esther/Rachel, who looks like either a slimmer version of Sarah Brightman or a chubby Sarah Jessica Parker.

The landscape was suggestive, hypnotic even. The sense that things haven't changed that much, especially away from the main roads, is palpable, a clammy ever-presence. The Time Team should employ a psychiatrist for this lot. This should have put me on my guard, the near geological persistence of the English Village. Its psychotic discontent, all Straw Dogs and Wicker Men. But at eighteen, full of spunk, fuck, it was going to be a blast.

The hunt protestors were gathered on the village green. The fucking toffs on horses surrounded us, nervously prancing with short stabbing trots going nowhere, skittering out on the tarmac in front of the pub, reined in by their masters as we chanted abuse. Hunting horns blared, taunting us with ancient notes. The locals spilled out from 'The Merry Monk', supping ale from their personal pewter mugs, jeering their feudal betters, performing the role of Greek chorus to the proceedings. The local coppers watched from the side-lines, exchanging banter with the locals. Cass's mouth flecked with spittle as she poured vitriol on the huntsmen. She really did see these people as her class enemy, let alone the animal welfare side of things. I couldn't help thinking that this was a further turn-off for me, as I cast furtive glances at her gob as she sprayed her saliva.

Five minutes later the stand-off was over and we were in trouble. The locals charged into the crowd whilst the fucking coppers popped into the pub for a drink. My reading of the rural working class and its state of political consciousness was misinformed. The first anti-hunt demo I go on and it looks like I'm going to get my head kicked in by the fucking Wurzels. Their betters soon joined in and it was open season on yours truly. I managed to smack some tosser in the side of the head with a stick, cunt looked like the Yorkshire Ripper, same shit clothes and sideburns. Hedged in on all sides, I watched in disbelief as ancient agendas were being negotiated in front of us, toffs on horseback, locals and beaters on foot laying into the mob. We didn't have a clue. Some student with green hair was taking a right pasting from a riding crop, his face looked like a child had scribbled red crayon all over it.

'Pull him off the fucking horse!' I screamed.

Green hair didn't have a clue and fell to the ground under the lash. The hunters retreated behind the men, masters of this universe overseeing the action. The few women on horseback I spotted must have been really wet between the legs looking down at us, posh cunt in the saddle. Head and shoulders above the village scrum, these were our liege lords, the country set, whose families, about thirty in all, run the whole fucking show. Now that's the real shit. So when a hundred or so of us 'troublemakers' turn up for this demo, fuck me, the ruling class and its cohorts were up for a fight, on home ground and spitting blood. Pity the fox? Pity the fucking anti-hunt protestor more like. We were chased off the green and into the woods, banners trampled underfoot. Mr. Fox was going to get the morning off. Shotguns loaded with salt blasted our arses all over the valley as we tried to escape. Sucking mud pulled us down, tree roots tripped, brambles ripped, as what seemed like the whole village chased us. The countryside had risen up once again to repel invaders, as pathetic as we were, our tactics non-existent. We had no boats waiting for us on the beach.

And they were athletic. Obviously the inbred sozzled gin addicts amongst them stayed at home. This lot were lean. Range Rovers came at us over fields as we scrabbled out of their way, up into the low branches of trees. Golf clubs, polo clubs, shotguns, beating sticks, they threw the lot at us. It was a total rout. Black flags trampled in the mud, Greenpeace banners set on fire, dykes dry-humped for laughs by Esquires of the Manor. What were we thinking? Dragging Cassy by the hand we managed to make it up onto the main road, leaving the rest in the valley below.

Bedraggled on the train home, I took stock. We had been kicked, beaten, spat at, abused, I saw one black protestor actually wanked on. The countryside is a fucking nightmare. Can you imagine what a shit time that money-lending Jew must have had with these people?

Back on campus we took stock of the day's events, each drew our own conclusions. On the news it was like a report on the same event in a parallel universe. They had even arrested some of the protestors. Cassy had got herself a bruised tit and a sprained ankle. I a bruised ego. She begged off further protest and eventually got a 2.1 degree in politics. I however was hooked. 'We' would have to up our game. The overclass had revealed their hand.

The People's Will

Zoos and Wildlife Parks offer themselves as prime targets. Not that we saw them as particularly cruel places, hamster or monkey farms were a lot worse, but that wasn't the point. It was the psychic damage I was interested in, the mind fuck of targeting these 'soft' targets. I had never been interested in any kind of 'Setting free the Bears' romanticism; although in that strange locus, the Venn diagram where humans and animals intersect, zoos put both circles at a disadvantage.

They were places that brought out the worst in both of us.

Years before our 'action' – see how readily the 'terminology' slips off the tongue – I visited the Cotswolds Wildlife Park. Two things, two incidents made me realise, wake up to, what was deeply wrong about what these places did.

At the leopard enclosure, which was a relatively big glass and steel space and had probably won many design awards, a dog was having what can only be described as a spastic fit of barking, slobbering and sporadically thrashing at the glass with his paws to get at the leopard within. His owner, a guy in his late fifties, just stood there staring at the leopard, which was 6 inches of glass away from his rabid dog. Now the leopard was responding in kind and then some, to how the dog was behaving. It was literally going berserk, hurling itself at the glass, smearing flecks of blood on it, which in turn enraged the dog even further. This cycle continued, I was surprised the leopard didn't knock itself out. Blood/saliva dripped down the glass on both sides. The owner of the fucking dog just stood there staring, seemingly fascinated, into the enclosure. Eventually somebody shouted in a very polite middle-class fashion for the man to take his dog away. He ignored them and they loudly muttered 'shame' in his general direction. Other people looked around nervously for zoo keepers.

Dog and leopard separated by a sheet of glass going apeshit at each other. It was like the dog knew he was safe from the cat. It was a Labrador for fuck's sake. The whole scene was like a twisted send up of Tom and Jerry.

Shame? This guy needed a good kick in. He looked at his watch and finally moved off, tugging the dog away. As he passed by I called him a cunt under my breath.

From there I went to see the lions. Again, another good-sized award-winning enclosure. A lazy male slumped on a small hummock of grass, doing absolutely nothing, in fact seeming to be making an effort to appear vastly underwhelming. I flashed on these cats doing the whole Lion-King spiel at night after all the kids, mums and dads had fucked off.

A couple of female lions were doing a little low-grade prowling up and down the perimeter ditch; repetitive pacing, to and fro, reminded me of the film *Shock Corridor*. Kind of autistic and repetitive, edgy, if you looked close enough. They were being watched by some families, who were obviously bored with the absence of spectacle these so-called lions were refusing to provide. Camcorders, digital cameras, disposable Kodaks bought from the novelty shop, all hung at half-mast.

It started to drizzle which I imagine the lions appreciated as much as the people. One little girl said to her mum, 'Don't they do anything mum?' She replied, 'Bit boring really aren't they dear, come on, we'll go and see the penguins.'

They left and sometime later the male lion roared/yawned. Some fucker clapped and three people raised up their cameras and started filming, obviously after the fact, in a consecutive sequence of events worthy of Beckett. An action, pause, click, action, pause, click, which is in essence what contemporary photography amounts to for the masses, capturing the dead spaces between events before deleting them.

I'd had enough by now and said to nobody in particular, but loudly, something I had picked up from the Discovery channel:

'If you are having a period apparently it drives the big cats crazy.'

I expected to hear mumbled shames or some-such, but no, no response, just a silent moving along.

I guess this fact is only relevant for people working with lions or if you live in a village somewhere where lions are 'in the wild'. Where the village, the hut, is in effect, the cage. Where these big cats can come and look at you, or eat ya!

In the movie business they have to use female lions for the action sequences because male lions are too lazy. So they put a wig mane on the females to make them look like males, because 'we', the gazing morons that are the US, expect the guy to be the vicious one, the go-getter. In real life, which I know is a contentious fucking notion at the best of times, the male lion will eat, fuck and sleep and that's about it. He won't try and maul Russell Crowe, or eat Christians, or run rampage 'cos that just ain't him. He may try and fuck up another male lion who's trying to steal his pussy, he may. But 'WE' still think he does all that stuff because THEY put wig manes on the female lions.

I met somebody one time who had worked on a movie that had lions in it, in Namibia. He told me a very cool story that hopefully will alleviate the above tale of our own species' duplicity and leaven the mock/horror impact of what is to follow.

This movie was a typical Hollywood number. They flew out a specialist lion trainer, a guy called 'Sledge' ('The sledge'), who had worked on Gladiator and The Ghost and the Darkness. He was the go-to guy when it came to 'big cats' on film. A real fucking cliché with the riding boots, the wide-brimmed hat, the crop, Mr. 'White Mischief' himself, somebody who had a twisted ownership psychology going on towards wildlife and 'big game' in particular. He really wanted to fuck wildlife, dominate nature, had a whole sado-sexual deal going on. And this is Namibia, home of FRELIMO, and the armed struggle against European exploitation. He should have been lynched.

The guy who told me the story was a lowly production

assistant to one of four producers on the gig. As well as lions there were a lot of horses in the film, so they brought over Navajo horse wranglers. Of course they did. I mean serious horse-whispering shit, these guys were a very different, authentic, cliché. In the context of pure exploitation and colonial style production, in which the locals were either dressed up like extras in Zulu or doing the catering, these four Navajo men and their horses were untainted. That's how it appeared to the production assistant, who had his own shit, his own soul to wrangle, his own circles of manageable pain to endure.

Every night he would seek these guys out by their fire. Suck up some of their calmness, smoke some of their insane weed. And Namibia is really fucking beautiful, especially at night when the sky appears as a vast velvet blanket sewn with diamonds.

The Navajo didn't seem to mind him, occasionally passing him a bottle or a spliff, but there seemed to be something he was missing out on, a joke he wasn't in on. The Indians exchanged looks, smiles and silences with each other, silences that sometimes lasted for hours. Six weeks into the shoot he plucks up enough courage to ask what's going on. One of them just shrugs and asks him what animal he dreamed of being. People who aren't Indians, and probably most Indians, don't dream about being animals enough to have an immediate and unself-consciously honest answer. So our guy said a bear, but after too long of a beat for this to bear the weight of any real truth. The Indian looked at him for a long time and the only thing he said was 'Too bad'.

A week later the film wrapped. Back in the capital Windhoek there was a big crew party. The Navajo were nowhere to be seen, but at the bar drunk and wobbly our assistant overheard the following conversation, as one of the grips told a tall tale.

'So we took the stuff, tasted bitter, with an odd heat underneath it. There was some chanting, an endless undertone, a bass kinda noise that underscored the whole shit, man it was fucking unreal, I felt my heart ballooning in my chest, but my chest expanded to contain it, at that point I was out of it, out of conscious constraint, I felt like a fucking horse, no, I was a horse, I had become a horse, fuck it's difficult to describe, my limbs grew muscle and sinew and I fucking pounded the ground, zoomed off, literally the ground just eaten up underneath me. I was there man, a fucking horse running over the endless plain under a velvet sky sprinkled with diamonds, with these crazy Indian horses running alongside me, a rippling moonlight reflecting off the sweat sheen of their dark coats. In-fucking-sane man. Insane!'

Sledge, the lion tamer was listening in, shaking his head, so fucking angry he missed out, liquor bubbling from behind his lips on to his safari shirt, his bad energy killed the whole evening. The assistant nodded to the grip, probably whispered 'Far out', he was that kind of guy.

Running horses across the endless Namibian plain under a velvet sky sewn with diamonds. That's where he got that description from and knew it to be true, and told me the story in a melancholic way, knowing that he had missed out on it. Shift shape.

Dog/glass/leopard.

So years later when we were discussing our first move, our inaugural intervention, wildlife parks, zoos, seemed to suggest themselves as an obvious target. We were an Anarchist group for fucks sake, informed by a strong strain of animal-liberation ideology.

Releasing Big Cats has to trump setting free the mice/mink in terms of making a splash no? And nobody really gives a fuck about guinea pigs. Hasn't got the tabloid draw of say a Siberian Tiger or a white Rhino. That was my argument. Shit, how was I to know then what trouble guinea pigs were to cause us later. But then, just as 'The People's Will' was getting under way, moving out of the purely theoretical realm, an English countryside seething with big game seemed like the right statement to be making. Our version, an updating if you will, of bringing the hell-on-earth of a Vietnamese village into the heart of Europe.

Zoos were a no-go from the start. Do you know how difficult breaking into one of those places is? The Cotswold Wildlife Park was easier, but that was just getting in. The animals were to prove a fucking nightmare. There were six of us on the night, as we doused the lights of the van by the side of the road. Nips of vodka all round.

Break a leg.

The smart part, and ironically what got us into the most hot water later, in terms of being seen as a terrorist threat, was that we had managed to hack into their security camera system and replace the live feeds with stills we took on a previous visit. It's way easier than it sounds if you have an internet connection and a lot of time on your hands. Believe me.

We found out later, of twenty-six cameras we fucked with only three were working that night anyway. Unprofessional wankers.

We got in the park over a fence, pretty easy really, and then made our way to the lion enclosure. One of us, Little Tom, (a tall guy called Peter) kept look out. We knew the guards routine because the week before one of the security guards found himself being chatted up in his local by 'Steffi', an oversexed Israeli 'student' (aka 'BuffTatiana' from our friends the 'Lil'Annefranks' in Jerusalem).

She kissed him a few times, squeezed his balls under the table and he spilled his guts about what a big job he had etc.

We had approximately fifteen minutes to break into the enclosure and let the lions out. We had practiced using bolt cutters on wire mesh beforehand, and we had brought with us a plank to extend over the enclosure wall into the lions' den so they could walk up it. Now I assumed that the lions would be asleep, that we would be back outside the park before they bothered walking the plank to freedom, if indeed they did bother. There was no way any of us would have to go into the enclosure. As the leader, instigator, whatever, I had to project confidence. I thought the publicity of the stunt itself would be enough for openers. I had thought about breaking into the leopard enclosure but this would have meant knocking down a wall and would have taken too long as the glass was probably unbreakable. Also the leopards were crazy.

So a hole in the fence and a plank into the lions' den it was. What could go wrong?

It was pretty dark so we couldn't see any lions, or hear them. Fast asleep, we all thought simultaneously, not a little relieved. Although there were other strange noises coming from the park, which spooked us; odd calls, croaks and scuffles, erratic groans. I mean working here must drive you up the wall. On top of that the smell was awful. Animals. No sooner had the plank been lowered into the enclosure across the moat, an enormous shadow leapt, scrabbled across it and bound out in to the open. No roar, nothing, like it had been waiting for just this opportunity. It bounded off in the direction of where Tom was keeping lookout by the fence. The rest of us called out to warn him. Too late. His scream was so full of horror and sheer surprise that it shut all the other wildlife up in an instant. The fucking lion had bitten his arm half off and then jumped through the hole to freedom. By the time we got to him Tom was already in shock, spasming, fucking blood everywhere, and eerily silent, he didn't say shit after that bloodcurdling scream. I grabbed him and we made our way out. The iron stench of his blood made me feel ill, it was too intimate a smell, like I was fucking him, which I suppose in some way I had. This guy should have been protesting outside Oxford Life Science with a placard, not messing with this shit. I just couldn't believe that the lazy lion who never roared, or the autistic pacing lion, had it in them. Bitches. Its docility was a mask. Like it was biding its time for a chance to escape, whistling idly, cooling its heels on the fucking parade ground until... I mean think about it, we were breaking into a prison, what the fuck did we expect. Well, I had expected the papers, the local rag, maybe a national tabloid, to write this up as a bit of a lark, that good old Larry the lion would be found safe and sound having slept through the whole thing. That's what I really thought deep down, but now I was smothered in blood, a guy shaking in my arms and four others screaming and sobbing in turns as the van swerved its way to the nearest A and E. I had heard stories of farm hands calmly taking their severed limbs into hospital, but it was three-thirty in the morning and the last thing Little Tom looked like was a fucking farmer. He was wearing a 'Peace Now' Mapam t-shirt, which means he had probably slept with 'BuffTatiana' damn it, combat boots and camo-trousers. His hair was dyed yellow and he had a scraggly beard. Under all the blood that is.

I hastily scribbled a note for the doctors and coppers, which I pressed into Tom's good hand as we left him in Emergency. Under the sodium glare he looked already dead. Smeared in blood it would make a great photo in the morning's papers, and had a direct symbolic, even literal tie-in with what we were about.

'A lion leaps to freedom. Captivity had not cowed its brute strength and dreams of freedom. This arm is testament to this first liberation. It will not be the last. Our blood has been spilt in a good cause. And yours?'

Signed 'The People's Will'.

Not bad, considering.

A few innocent asthmatics waiting for their nebulisers shrieked when they saw this war wound and Tom was quickly surrounded by nurses. I ducked out and we made best our getaway.

Somehow on the ride away from the hospital and during the drinking of at least three bottles of vodka during a frenzied autopsy of events I didn't think this had been a great start to our little insurgency. Little was I to know that within months, thanks in part to the scum-sucking press, teenagers throughout the country would be tying one arm behind their backs in solidarity with our actions, a blind Home Secretary would seek to extend the law on animal rights activism, and little Tom, god bless him, he was getting more pussy than he could ever have dreamt of.

The Jain Meal

So I have to fly this mucky muck over from LA for a screening of my film. Not only did the fucking thing cost me sixty grand to shoot, but this big-shot has to be flown Premium Economy to view it. 'We love the reel.' Another two grand. 'Be great to see the film.' Jesus. The film's only twenty minutes long. I should get a real job. But you need bait to go fishing, 'in for a penny, in for a pound' and blah blah blah, I find myself on the internet booking this studio mid-shot a Premium Economy ticket on my Amex; a real come-down for him, believe me, he let me know he was doing me a favour not traveling Upper, or to be more precise his PA let me know that it's not part of his 'usual itinerary', but he really wants to see the film on the big screen…

One of the bullshit parts of my job is having to watch fucking short films directed by bullshit commercials directors who think they are the next big thing. They have great reels for sure, but where are their big ideas? Usually their films are just so much wannabe LA bullshit. A sexy girl, a stripper or a happy hooker, a suitcase of cash or coke, a seedy motel room in a bum-fuck nowhere town and perhaps an old Indian guy full of wisdom at the gas station. Thousands of times I've had these films on my desk. Who do these idiots think we are? This is America already? Rundown hotels and bags of stolen money? But I watch them. It comes with the territory. Junior VP of an ex-indy movie company trying to punch at studio weight. So I find myself being flown to London, hey my boss won't pay, but at least I'm showing willing. It's a free trip, to see a short film directed by somebody I never heard of, but at least it's a different type of script, he sounded nice on the phone, comes with a few ok recommendations, on Virgin Premium Economy. Nice. Ish. There are some other people I need to see in town anyway, blah blah blah. As soon as I check in I smell a fucking rat. That's funnier than it sounds, bear with me.

Booking the flight I come across the drop-down option box

for meal preferences. I click and find sixteen options ranging from vegetarian/vegan to Kosher to Hindu to gluten-free to Muslim. In this list is a double-word option. Jain Meal. What does that mean? Something strange for sure. So you know what? I find myself clicking it. Fuck him! American cunt, let him eat Jain. As soon as the flight was booked, I felt that sickening feeling in my stomach after you send an angry/drunk/true email. I couldn't take it back. There was no postman on his collection round to stalk and mug. This electronic irretrievable sending is terrible. I sat there deflated and knew that I was just another chip-on-his shoulder Englishman always prepared to bite the American hand that might just possibly feed him. Great. Maybe he would think it was just a booking error. Maybe.

'Everything's fine sir, your special meal preference is all booked in, go right ahead and board the plane.' Special meal preference? What? Has this English director somehow googled that I like Osso-fucking-Bucco? Or booked me champagne and caviar blinis to make up for the Premium Economy thing? I doubt if that's possible. Anyway I let it pass and get on the plane, after all the Upper Class winners, I made a right turn at the door. Actually the new Premium Economy is nice, more leg-room, leather chairs, great in-flight service, I mean who in their right mind would ever pay out the thousands extra for Upper Class? For a narrow flat bed. But I see them all up there, turn left at the door, up the stairs and straight ahead and they don't just look like corporate guys on the companies coin, there's also the once-in-a-lifetime tourists, retirees doing London/Europe/LA in style, men and women sitting Kitty Kat to each other, or cramming themselves into the foot-stall seat of their spouse's flat-bed, clinking cheap champagne cocktail glasses at whatever goddamn hour they get on the plane, paying way over the odds for fizzy wine and disco music. Fuck them. I sit back, drink some OJ and read Variety.

Jain. A weirdo Indian sect? They have to be more than a cult to appear on a Virgin Atlantic drop-down option menu. Branch Davidian isn't an option, although what would that have stipulated? Waffle house? Jack in the Box? Why is a sect not a cult, what's the difference? At what point do either of these become a religion? Is it just a question of numbers, is that what gives belief validity? Jains. An extreme branch of Hinduism perhaps? Not knowing what this means bugs me. I google it. Jain Dharma. Its full name. An ancient pacifist/spiritual religion that believes in the equality of all life, non-violence and freedom of belief. Their central symbol is a simple swastika. I repeat that awkward sentence to myself. A simple swastika. Doesn't sound right to my European sensibility. The possibility that this word, this shape can have any anterior meaning than the obvious. So I'm intrigued, I want to know more. Didn't Jack Kerouac once write a book called *The Dharma Bums*? I have no recollection of what it was about. Jains? Most Jains are strict vegans. Hence the meal option. At least I have an idea what the studio guy is going to get to eat. Hahaha.

Dinner is served. The hostess stands in front of me holding a tinfoil covered meal.

'What is it?' I ask.

'The Jain meal sir, as requested.'

The words 'a Jain meal' could have been anything, she had no idea what they meant, they contained no meaning for her and you could hear this absence of meaning in the words as they sat in the sentence between 'The' and 'sir' and 'as requested'. Instead of saying I didn't order a Jain meal, or that there must be some mistake, or I'll eat anything etc., for some reason I asked her what was it again.

'Your Jain meal', *the hapless girl replied.*

She was stuck and I wasn't going to help her.

'I have no idea what that is, what's in it?'

'I don't know sir.'

'Well I'm not going to eat something if I don't know what it is.'

She peels back the tinfoil to reveal a risotto, porridge-type sludge. Neither of us are any wiser as to what it is. I look up at her.

'It gets specially delivered onto the plane sir by outside caterers.'

'So it could be anything?' I say.

We've come a long way from a Chicken or Pasta option, but nobody seems to have learnt anything. The hostess turns towards the galley and shouts.

'Mike do you know what's in a J meal?'

He shakes his head and turns back to serving his customer the filet mignon on a bed of potato and chicory mash. The Jain meal had now become the J meal; it was tamed, and I was just a nuisance passenger. Its teeth had been pulled, despite not knowing what it meant, the meal itself was now corralled, tied up and pacified as the J meal. One of many, one of a sequence of possible meals to serve, the A,B,C,D,E,F,G,H,I or J meal. Or did I just mishear her say Jain. These long flights extend and complicate our thought processes. Hey we can do without a meal right, it's no biggie.

Jains had a big influence on the beliefs of Ghandi. The word means victors. Those who can liberate themselves from their bodies, thereby achieving the perfectibility of man. They are also the most literate group in India and the most philanthropic. They run lots of free schools and hospitals. They believe in karma and karmic reincarnation being based upon what we each do in this and every life we lead. Einstein once said he wanted to come back as an Indian Jain. Their word for bad karma is 'paap'. Like when we say something is pap, i.e. rubbish. How on earth did that get into the English lexicon? I cancel a meeting in order to read more about Jains.

I was hungry, there must have been some mix up with the meal although the hostess stubbornly showed me that I had been booked in as a Jain meal. I persuaded them I wasn't a Jain by showing them my Amex platinum company card and they gave me a left-over linguini vongole, although how wise is it to eat shellfish at 35,000 feet above sea level? I snooze and wonder about the asshole who booked my flight and the film I'm going to see; A dark rural tale of guinea pig farms and animal rights extremism...

Strict Jains wear veils not out of modesty but in order to

protect insects from flying into their mouths and getting killed. I shit you not. They don't even eat root vegetables because so doing destroys, eradicates a whole plant. Apples and stuff that drops or can be picked off plants and trees is OK. Their monks brush the ground in front of them, not out of vanity but in order to protect small animals or plants from getting walked on. This image is weirdly moving to me. The screaming animal rights protestors in my short film have an unlikely ally in these Jains.

Unedited sequences of bad action movies, which is what I call the dreams I have been experiencing lately, leave me with a headache and a sense of not having had enough sleep. The hostess places a tray in front of me.

'Your special breakfast sir.'

I get served before everyone else. It's like I'm an embarrassment, or what I eat is, or that they are scared of me. Like a food terrorist. The disgusting porridge/broth that no doubt awaits me under the tinfoil another two finger-lickin' good salute to American values. Eat this buddy! I'm fully awake and sit up in my chair. The Jain breakfast. You gotta be kidding me. Again I ask her,

'What is it?'

Again she says she has no idea what's in the J meal, that it comes onto the plane direct from the outside caterer.

'Isn't that a security risk?' I ask, gingerly peeling back the tinfoil. Maybe it will explode? She blinks slowly and goes and gets me an orange juice. I notice the swish of her tights and crane my neck to see her visible stocking line. Nice. Now you don't get that on US Air and nor would you want it.

Jain thought has cross fertilised with Sikhism, Hinduism and Buddhism for thousands of years. It underpins many of their beliefs, as it predates those religions to the sixth century. The Jain ethical code is simple yet very powerful. Non-violence, truth, non-stealing, chastity for monks and non-possession. Or in a slight bending of their ascetic values, non-possessiveness. Individual believers can attain salvation by passing through nine levels, nine 'Tatvas' of Jain belief. Every birth, every reincarnation is aimed at being the last when the spirit can transcend the body and they achieve true Mohksha, realisation of the soul's true nature.

Again a strange resonance with English slang, 'Tatva' reminds me of 'tat' in the phrase 'tit for tat'. This for that. What if some cockney sailor or soldier went to India during the Raj and became friendly with a Jain monk? Now that would be a great movie. I stay at my desk and continue my research, ignoring the phone.

We land. Just as I'm about to get off the plane the hostess who served me gestures me into the back.

'It's about the Jain meal sir. I've just looked it up on my phone. They're Indians, vegetarians, like a cult I think.'

'There must be a lot of them for their food preference to appear on a Virgin booking form.'

'Yes, there are a lot of Indians, I suppose some of them must be Jains.'

'Great, thanks for the info.'

'Have a great day sir.'

At that moment the penny drops. It must have been that English fucker. An example of the famous Brit humour. Cheap cunt was pissed at having to shell out a coupla grand for my flight. I'm sick of English dicks who travel coach to LA and think they are saints, or as I can say now, Jains. Oy vey I hate this guy's movie already...

Sweet Jain. Forbidden love under the Raj. A lowly British subaltern falls in love with the teenage daughter of Jain businessman in Lahore. Maybe I'll pitch this idea to the yank coming to see my film. At least he'll be acquainted with their food.

It's funny that Jains are amongst the wealthiest of Indians, despite, maybe because of, their asceticism. That's the difference between non-possession and non-possessiveness I guess. And you can say anything you want to about them, what they believe and they won't try and kill, defame or abuse you. Now that's scary. A religion that is so self-confident, so assured of its beliefs that whatever you say or do to it doesn't elicit a response other than the continued preaching of its beliefs and extending an understanding of yours. Think about what that means.

Jain philosophy states that ultimate salvation comes by shedding Karma. That's when you release yourself from the shackles of worldly existence, into a universe which will never cease and was never created but has always been. There is no God, but this universal spirit, which by our own actions we can contribute to. By achieving Siddha. When we become like gods, in fact the Indian panoply of gods, Siddhartha included, are revealed as metaphors, examples of those that have succeeded in the pure release of their individual spirit, the final shedding of the human veil. How on earth guinea pigs can do this I don't know, but the fact that they can in Jain world makes me smile as I watch the opening credits to my film roll. A packed house, hands grasping complimentary drinks.

Two seats back that yank is watching the film, I try not to catch his eye until after the screening. I hope he enjoyed his flight.

Girl on a Bridge

Pirajoux

The middle of a hot endless summer, driving on the A39 through an, as always, empty central France, which exudes as always a certain seventies timelessness. The anxiety of being in a Ballard novel, the feeling of a certain narrative disconnectedness, that anything could happen or not, at the stroke of a pen. And that whether something happens or not is somehow equally as disastrous an outcome. But not knowing who or what the subject of this disaster would be, if anyone or anything.

This is what shrinks call free-floating anxiety, I guess.

Poulet De Bresse

Passing unseen towns, picnic areas, petrol stations and auto-grills, crawling along at 100 miles an hour, the faster you go the slower it all gets, chastened by the knowledge that a slight jerk to the right or left would speed everything up again and end your life in a chaos of twisted steel, spilt petrol and screaming children. The promise of an almost sci-fi shift in motion, a quantum leap, an ion drive surge tugs at the edges of this mundane driving reality. Wildly fraying threads spastically unspooling at the edges of perception.

The death-defying habits of the open road...

Hands alternately sweating, slipping on the wheel, followed by air-con clamminess, never finding the right balance of temperature to stop this yawing between discomforts; eyes lingering too long on the climate controls, fiddling with them, changing the flow, exasperated turning the A/C off and cracking the window. Sweating feet in Birkenstocks; damn their eyes a more prosaic way to die I couldn't think of than this continual loss of concentration on the road due to adjusting dials and vents. More dialling through French radio stations, one French song, one

American song, the bipolarity of taste and rhythm leaving you in the purgatory of always changing stations; Melodie, Nostalgie, Virgin, Classique, Energie.

Cuiseaux

Pulling in to a 'Croq Malin' forecourt concession for lunch, leaving the car behind, clicking to itself in the heat. Feet squelching towards the services, as we swamp the self-service restaurant, devouring the ersatz gastronomy from whatever region we are currently in. A vague notion of identity predicated on cuisine, memories of cherished recipes and hand-crafted artisan foods. All of these re-represented along the self-service counters, dispelling any fear of the land of hunger. And don't forget the tokens for the coffee machine, or you will have to rejoin the queue or brave the displeasure of your fellow diners by hovering by the check-out, apologetically alternating gestures between the coffee machine, the check-out person and the till, where you imagine the tokens are dispensed from.

Phew. Back on the road…

Lorries and caravans slide by through the treacle on your right-hand side, a few feet yet thankfully a parallel universe away. A hand-turn away, a jerk on the wheel to the right, the everyday power that's in your hands: 'the hand that signed the paper fell'd the city' type of power. What I'm getting at I suppose is a heightened sense of contingency, that one thing depends on another, and that certain things have to be just so for other things to be as they are. And that everything can change just like that, or that you think you can make things stay as they are by an effort of will.

Savigny

Hot gusts of wind, blustery siroccos channelled by miles of super-heated tarmac and concrete; heat secreted by everything, amplified, bounced between structures, surfaces distorting the flow of air, sculpting vortices and random spikes of temperature, tunnels of hot air magnified, concentrated by bridges and autoroutes, fly-overs, bypasses and industrial suburbias, advertising hoardings and signage, neon, paint, metalled surfaces and deserted forecourts populated by ranks of as-yet unsold shiny new cars and vans.

Heat and air shaped as if on a potter's wheel.

Louhans

A woman stands on the outside of the railings on a bridge over the motorway. She is barefoot, her shoes and trainers sit side by side next to her. The hot wind buffets her, her red hair flies in front of her face and her hand comes up to tuck the loose strands back behind her ear. She leans into the wind over the tarmac below, scanning the road for an oncoming lorry. I see all this as I pass under the bridge at 90 miles per hour; I register it in less than three seconds. 75 frames of information, of story, recorded on a French motorway at the end of our summer holidays.

My wife saw the same thing, the kids saw nothing. I started to say 'did you see that…' but got as far as 'did you' when my wife's shaking head cut me off. We didn't talk about it properly until late the same night back in London: an unsatisfactory conversation, a strange end-of-holiday conversation, awkwardly passing over in silence what should be talked about.

A pair of trainers, Adidas laces flickering in the wind.

Three stripes and the candle goes out…

The next day I googled 'suicide autoroute France' and found nothing.

If she took a dive off the bridge, which would in reality not be a dive as such, but just a drop, much faster, over and done, some 'beautiful dive into eternity' or whatever, timed right to fall under the wheels of an oncoming Lorry, what the fuck would have happened next? Would the driver just plough on? Or screech to a halt, parallel black wobbly rubber smears veering off the road like a lazy eye, adrenalin jump down from his cab into the searing heat and look back to see precisely what? Cars swerving to avoid what was left of the girl, swerving onto the hard shoulder and into the driver crushing him in his moment of surprise/grief, and on and on, until at what point would everything set in motion by this dive, this falling come to a rest, when would it all stop and what would it look like?

The last frame of this sequence. Paint it for me. What would it look like?

Could this chain of events really be endless, achieve an endlessness of motion, a pile-up of the whole of humanity, at least the part of it that throws itself down autoroutes every summer? We seem to be back in a Ballard story.

I have a fantasy or a memory of 9/11, of a guy standing with his back to a blazing room high up in one of the towers, taking a laconic last drag on his cigarette before flicking it nonchalantly, fuck-you nonchalantly, into the abyss, following it with nothing more than a simple foot forward. I think I made this up. Or was told it was footage from a Mexican news crew that was banned so no-one saw it. Go on and youtube 'man cigarette 9/11', or 'cool guy 9/11 cigarette' or 'Mexican news footage', 'guy 9/11', 'cigarette', 'last drag', 'flicked stub', whatever. I will, to see whether I did make it up or discover that I share this fantasy with somebody else, in the community of narrative fantasy that makes up/populates/clogs the internet.

Maybe a Platonic web search using the words 'last cigarette' would immediately hit this lost/imaginary footage, link us to this 'Bonny and Clyde' moment, the greatest cigarette commercial ever, featuring the Marlboro man and his nonchalant last flick.

But my girl was on the bridge, I did see her, but she just googled blank.

Most likely she jumped, got run over and the lorry/car/van managed to pull up without further impact, and the cars behind just kept going, a few passenger-seat twisted heads and backseat faces pressed up to the glass as the drivers kept going, always forward onward into their very own next chapters and not stopping to witness somebody's last. So cars flash past as the lorry driver stumbles about on the hard-shoulder just staring at what's left of her, gagging, dialing the police on his mobile, cars now nimbly avoiding the mess. Perhaps somebody else does stop and asks the driver if he's alright, a conversation screamed by the side of the road, or the driver just sits in his cab blasting the air-con as everything burns outside, on the other side of the glass. His fear-sweat drying almost as soon as it perspires, repeating the circuit between car and body, waiting for the police to turn up and sort it out, not wanting to see what had happened, horns blaring smearing up and out, back to front, in shock horror as cars go by outside accusing him in some way, so that he takes refuge behind the glass of his cab. The windshield itself could have been cracked if the girl's timing had placed her momentarily on the windscreen of the lorry, or bouncing from the bonnet into the windscreen, a flying visit too brief to leave any other sign than that of impact, the body tossed aside in the space of a second, a ragdoll discarded, the driver squeezing the wheel in automatic response not to swerve and crash, just ploughing straight on until he recovers his bearings, not swerving losing control in an attempt to avoid something that has already happened, like so many drivers who kill themselves and their families for the sake of a rabbit or a deer.

How hair blowing in your face can be annoying; you reach up to clear it away, put it back in place, so that you can see what you are doing. A great adrenalin rush as you lean into the wind, away from the railings, anchored only by your fingertips. Hot metal sticking to pads of flesh. A sense of freedom; freedom from the heat, the stifling provincial heat, toes curl cool and dry released from their sticky trainers, hair as you know, blowing about, you do this every day wondering what the people in the cars below think you are doing and who you are, how terrible if one of them lost control of their caravan car or lorry just because they were looking up at you wondering if you were going to throw yourself off and instead they crashed and killed themselves and their kids and you lean sharply back in, hiding from view, vault back across the railings and creep in dread to the other side of the bridge to see what you had done.

Now that was the real thrill. To find out if you had become a murderer.

'...The so called "Siren of the Motorways" is suspected of causing the deaths of 15 people across central France. Appearing about to jump to her death from overpasses and bridges she draws the eye of those passing below. Sightings have been reported from across the country...'

The rush of emotion and energy that leads to the bridge, to the parapet, the edge, is the same that keeps my eye on the road and my hand on the wheel. We are all vessels for this flow and containment of feeling, urges, the fluctuating will to live or to die. Imagine a pyramid of empty champagne glasses in a ballroom or a casino. The waiter pours a magnum of champagne which cascades from the apex glass down into all the others, spilling, bubbling, vomiting over each successive glass; that's us, we are like those glasses in a pyramid, the girl on the bridge somewhere near the top maybe, unable to contain her juices, and me, the rest of us, somewhere lower down where the flow is less intense and the containment more manageable, the spillage more pragmatic. It takes a lot of us to keep the others, the few, up. To support the apex.

Heading back into the village she doesn't look back, the sound of cars recedes almost too quickly, depositing her back in the vast empty world of rural France. Time to pick her kid up from her grandmother's house. Nobody ever notices me, she thinks, nobody looks up, I might as well jump for all anybody cares. A stupid way to insert yourself in the world; a clumsy intervention, but how else to enter the stream, how else? Ten minutes later the child's hand reaches out for hers and won't let go all the way home, and she realises that for the child she is the stream, how stupid and selfish she is, and she won't go anywhere near that damn bridge again, but had better learn how to swim all by herself, in order someday to teach the child ways to survive in this land of endless hunger.

Prefixed

Prefix (def): a type of affix that precedes the morphemes.

'Raspberry please mate, yeah, two scoops, thanks.'

It was a predictably hot afternoon on somewhere like Santa Monica beach front. I say 'somewhere like' because there are no distinguishing features to this stretch of sea-front, there's a boardwalk and a pier but that's pretty generic really to quite a lot of coastline. The guy ordering an ice-cream is with a film crew, who we can see on the beach. He is in fact the director. So this is the most defining feature of the landscape that puts us somewhere specific. A film crew is a pretty specifically organised entity, it has a regular shape to it, a consistent hierarchy; in fact it occupies a definitive cultural, economic space within the wider framework of late-capitalist production. Looking closer at this guy, in his early forties, but dressed six or seven years younger, a look which itself is a good ten years younger again, is typical of the type of person you would see at the apex of a film crew. A middle-aged guy dressed like a teenager. He has paint on his trainers, Jackson Pollock splashes that don't come from this guy painting in his spare time or DIY but are sold as such; the paint is an expensive add-on to the pair of jeans. He has lots of bangles and tied bits of string on his wrists, a yellow plastic 'Live-Strong' bracelet, the badge d'honneur of this specific class of person before Lance Armstrong fucked it all up. He has messy hair, a little greasy, expensive glasses and a funny slouch that says I don't give a fuck about anything, I am a creative person. Looking at him, my nan would probably say he should get over himself. But if somebody pointed him out to you as the director you wouldn't be surprised or raise an eyebrow and exclaim 'What, him?' in disbelief. He fulfils certain expectations of his job, performs well the function of himself. Suffice it to say the guy isn't black or a woman.

Serving him on the other hand is somebody you would also not disbelieve if the same person who pointed out the director said, 'look that guy over there manning the ice-cream float, yeah the young Mexican guy, he's the ice-cream guy'.

This story happens in what is called a break in filming. It's mid-afternoon, so it's not lunch, and there is activity down on the beach where a 'shot is being set up' which involves the laying of boards and track and the building of a dolly with a crane arm, the positioning of monitors and a tented shaded area for the agency; meaning advertising agency. So this is a TV-commercial shoot and not a movie shoot, although to all intents and purposes they look the same. As always happens after lunch the crew is a little sluggish from eating too much rib-eye, T-bone, New-York-strip steak and everything takes longer than it did in the morning to get going. It's boring for the director who has to stand around and wait, not a good thing as you will see. This director has in fact said, is on record as saying, that when he shoots a movie the catering will be vegetarian.

Meanwhile on the beach and the pier a few sight-seers gather, I want to say congeal like pooling blood in the extremities of a cadaver, but that would be a little much. These tourists stop, stare and point looking for the inevitable celebrity, whilst others, probably locals, casually rollerblade by and elsewhere the homeless sun themselves under the palm trees, veterans' prosthetic limbs expanding in the heat beside them. It's all part of the mix.

The director has decided to go and get himself an ice-cream. To kill time. Now that is unusual in itself because directors on shoots don't have to get themselves anything. They have runners and PAs to get them stuff. So this guy, obviously a Brit with a chip on his shoulder about being served and waited on, i.e. he hates it, such sycophantic treatment goes against the grain of his socialist ideas and democratic sensibilities, wanders over to the

ice-cream stall and orders his favourite flavour, two scoops of
rich dark-red raspberry in one of those old-fashioned thick wafer
spirals that look like edible layers of flaky slate. He turns away
from the guy to talk to what probably is his producer. I imagine
he has asked her if she wants one too, because she came over
from the beach after he ordered his ice-cream. She declines,
nervously looking down at her watch. He turns back to the
vendor who hands him a cone with two big scoops of pale-green
pistachio.

'Sorry, I asked for raspberry.'

He doesn't take the offending pistachio cone, which hangs
there over the counter in the Mexican guy's hand. Instead he
gestures by way of explanation to the raspberry tray.

'You said Pistachio.'

'I didn't, I said raspberry, I pointed to it. I want a raspberry ice
cream, I fucking hate Pistachio.'

By now the ice-cream is starting to run down the sides of the
cone, towards the man's hand, a ticking clock on the resolution of
this stand-off. Mistakes like this must happen in all forms of
exchange; on the phone, in shops, even online, there are misun-
derstandings, one person says something, the interlocutor hears
something else. Orders get confused, it's built in, hardwired into
the very nature of exchange, in fact these miscommunications,
interpersonal cock-ups, are an everyday heartbeat of human
activity whether social, sexual, commercial or whatever.

Perhaps it was the director's British accent that threw the guy,
made him hear pistachio instead of raspberry, yet if you try it,
say the two words out loud, it's hard to get a transposition out of
those two very dissimilar words, they don't even have the same
syllables, pistachio, raspberry. Now the only question we could
add on a linguistic level is does the fact that the other guy's first
language is Mexican-Spanish have any impact on how he hears
Brit-inflected English. I have no idea. I wouldn't think so, I am
not familiar with Spanglish.

Because this is a story, you have read in black and white that the guy asked for raspberry because I wrote it down on the first line. In this narrow sense it's a fact, there's no apparent mystery. But outside of 'words on the page' it is entirely possible that the director asked for pistachio flavour by mistake. I mean he opened his mouth and said pistachio even though he wanted to say raspberry, for whatever reason, whether just a slip of the tongue (I say 'just', slips of the tongue are the subject of whole schools of psychoanalytic study, of literary theory even), or something more clinically profound like say Apraxia. More importantly and above all, he thinks he said raspberry. Why wouldn't he?

So now he's being hassled by his producer to get back to work, to 'line up the next shot' or talk to the agency about a 'wardrobe issue'. She runs the clock and wants to move things on. Her big bugbear, the shibboleth of her life, is overtime, the incurring of which will kill any production-company markup it is her job to amass. What the director wants to do is get his raspberry ice-cream.

'Look, it doesn't matter, my mistake, I'll pay for both, just give me a raspberry one ok?'

He hands the guy a five-dollar bill. Ice-creams cost $2.50 each so five is the right money for two. The ice-cream vendor is still holding the pistachio cone in one hand, and takes the money with the other. By now he has a thin trail of pale-green pistachio running over his hand. Kind of goes with the territory. Getting sticky fingers from ice-cream is what happens if you sell ice-creams all day in the boiling heat, also getting ice-cream all over your money is going to happen too, so it must get in your trousers, everywhere actually, so when you go home you are a sticky guy and have to take a bath first thing before sitting down and getting your furniture and stuff sticky too. Driving home could be a bit tricky but hey, it's the job.

So 'Fuck you man' is not what you expect the guy to say next.
'What?'

'Fuck you, you never asked for raspberry.'

'You stupid cunt, just give me a fucking raspberry ice-cream.'

Now most Americans, by which I mean white middle-class people in general and white middle-class film types in particular, have an innate animal sense of how privileged their lives are and some part of them is always reminding them, warning them that 'There but for the grace of God go I' so don't ever provoke a 'Have Not' or else they might notice you and pick you out from the sublime anonymity of 'The Haves' for revenge.

Most Americans wouldn't call a young Mexican guy a stupid cunt. That ain't playing the game. The rules of which are dictated in silence. Politeness, an 'Aw shucks what a lottery life is' self-depreciating demeanor, domestic deference to waiters and all menial staff and general looking the other way, enables you to take all the spoils whilst everybody else cleans up, waits, parks your car and waters your beautiful flower-beds. This silence is full of words that crucially include the first name of the waiter/cleaner/gardener and maybe even their wife's and kids' names. This ownership of names guarantees the silence, these words of familiarity securely anchor this universe. Giving up your name on the other hand is in fact an act of the most obscene collusion. The moment you do it, the moment you exchange first names, heralds a celebration of enslavement more subtle and terrifying than any iron shackle, any whipping, castration, or any limb dismemberment you care to remember from history classes.

You don't call the help 'stupid cunts' unless you hold a bull whip and are prepared to use it. The whip that has been replaced in the main by the discrete and complex apparatus I have just outlined, so this Brit, this stupid cunt, who does he think he is coming here and lecturing us about our problems, this fucker has gone and upset the apple-cart. The rules went clear over his head. The Mexican's eyes harden, no longer those of an ice-cream vendor but of an angry young man. Pay me shit wages to park a car I couldn't afford in a hundred years, but don't call me a cunt, which is even ruder in American than in English, surprisingly able to communicate its granular medieval sense of sexual obscenity. The Mexican guy drops the ice-cream and chucks the money back at the director.

'Fuck you bitch.'

The ice-cream trolley between them has now for all intents and purposes disappeared, along with the disguise of ice-cream vendor. It is irrelevant, which in light of what the director does next is nothing if not ironic.

The producer meanwhile, up to this point, has seen the potential for trouble and has called up security on her walkie-talkie. This is her job, usually it involves driving the drunk director home, or even getting him hookers, or coke, she's his bitch basically, even if it just means taking him out to lunch/dinner every night of the shoot and picking up the tab without a thank you from him it's just what's done, part of the deal, the tab is not really on her personally but on the job, so everything is taken care of in an unsaid manner, of course because this is how social relations are carried out successfully these days under these conditions. Which is basically silence. Don't speak about it, don't mention it, don't for fuck's sake joke about it because any attention drawn to the rules ruins the smooth working of the machine. So this director guy who when he's on a job doesn't pay for jack shit, wanted to buy himself an ice cream with his own money, well with his 'per diems' to be precise, which is another hand-out from 'the job' that he's on and not his own money, that is kept for keeping the cunt alive for the other 350 days he isn't on a job, this freak – really we can call him that now, a freak who is paid a year's money for a few days' work, so is actually more lost than the guy selling the ice-cream but who no doubt would swap places with him in the bat of an eye – this Brit who is mightily pissed off with being waited on hand-and-foot, who finds it all so terribly claustrophobic and plain annoying, is now really fucked off that he's having a row with a guy who refused him the right ice-cream even after paying for it twice, what does he actually do next?

'Stupid cunt!'

He reaches over the small glass partition and tips the ice-cream tray all over the boardwalk, all over the Mexican guy. The whole thing is upended and crashes to the floor, if ice-cream can actually crash, but you get the picture. The Mexican has been reminded of his enslavement, his inscription in the story of America as an ice-cream seller, by having some Brit throw the fucking contents of the cart all over him. He stands there, in plain view, covered in ice-cream.

Both men of few words, they now proceed along the boardwalk, the one chased by the other. The film crew is at this point itself rendered irrelevant. They stare at each other thinking all the unsaid things that cause the machine to tremor. The director has run off chased by a Mexican and the grips, sparks, craft services, agency sit and contemplate how much the other guy is getting paid. The producer has taken off after them followed in third place by security who lag behind due to problems of excess weight.

Before this situation resolves itself, which it does inevitably, within a few minutes, it is not going be a long-distance chase, there is one question I would like to ask. The fact that I have come to it last is itself part of the answer. Following the rules of the 'Hierarchy of Silence' the main character of this story is the white guy, the guy on top, the guy with the film crew. Have I described what clothes the ice-cream vendor was wearing? No. What clues have I given to his personality other than his ethnicity? None. I don't know the ironies involved in the life of an ice-cream vendor on Santa Monica or wherever beach but I can vividly imagine them. So why didn't I six pages or so ago? Why did this guy get so hung up on not giving the Brit the ice-cream that he ordered? Even when he said he'd pay for the one he didn't want? Come on, this must happen all the time. This guy must have bills to pay, he must want to sell ice-creams. He knows it ain't the best job in the world, but he decided to turn up so why oh why make a scene, why not take the five bucks and scoop out the raspberry ice cream? A liberal story would have this as the moment of resistance, the moment when the underdog finally bites back but in such a pathetic fashion that the story ends bathed in pathos and terrible regret for life's terrible thumbscrew inevitability. In fact in the last scene of this story the ice-cream guy would be shot down by a jittery or blithely racist cop who sees a white guy being chased by a Mexican who may or may not be holding a knife, whereas in fact it's a scoop. In short, a tragedy. In another more contemporary postmodern story, the one which would get optioned to be a movie, we would discover that the Brit has been banging the guy's teenage sister and he recognised him when he came up to buy an ice-cream, in fact his sister met the director because she visited her brother by the pier after college and was cast in the commercial by a passing agent.

But my story isn't a story at all, in fact it's a dream. An anxiety dream, variations of which I always get the night before a shoot. So this dream is also an admission. In my dream what happens next is rather confused and doesn't abide by the rules and regulations of time and space. The director and the close members of his crew, i.e. his assistant, cameraman and producer, are all hiding out in a hotel room, giggling, still full of the adrenalin rush of having pushed over the ice-cream cart. Now in the dream an illogical shift occurs in which all of them were involved in pushing the guy's cart over. They planned it together, kind of. Now film crews pride themselves on the ability to solve problems, whether it's to do with the weather, a tricky location, a script that doesn't work, bad dialogue, bad acting, all these things are overcome by a good crew and the final film is always great, ok, whatever, but they are very good at avoiding disasters. The reason for this is the obscene amounts of money they get paid and that if they allowed a fuck-up to happen then the game would be up and they'd have to get a regular job. This is an example of extreme privilege that is unusual in that it focuses ability and creativity, and doesn't promote idle mediocrity. There is a meritocracy of sorts working in this industry. What this says about the mellifluous seduction of late capitalism is another story, but in the dream, in the next scene, and if you will indulge me, we cut to the British director who you by now have guessed is 'loosely' based on the writer, shaking hands with the Mexican guy who's been paid off and we fade on this resolution where everything bad has been smoothed over. In my mind the word 'prefixed' pops up at the end of the dream, starting with a thought of the sentence 'I'm going to fix myself a sandwich', a hokey old-fashioned American-English phrase I imagine that fantasy American dads would say to their respective wives and kids, as in 'I'm a fix myself a sandwich, any you's want one?'

Now as we have learnt already, directors and producers have runners and PAs who fix everything for them, from food to drink to drugs to chicks, everything is already sorted out, the hotel mini-bar bill is covered. The ubiquitous platinum American Express card has already sorted it. Every conceivable outcome, expenditure, within reason, within the parameters of the great silence, is covered by corporate credit. A scary thing in itself but nonetheless the fix is in, the handshake, the glossed-over incident, the calming restorative effect of money, the balance that it restores, even if under extreme pressure, so much so that the card itself is virtually molten from its kinetic exertions, like so much oil pumped into the San Andreas fault to keep the tectonic plates happy, all this condensed itself in my now waking mind into the word image 'prefixed'. I want to make a sandwich but a runner has already fixed it for me. The anxiety of this sentence is what promoted my dream into a story. Got it an upgrade into the wide awake.

There is a play here on the term prefix I'm sure but as with all dreams it doesn't yet deal in irony. Irony is still the preserve of the waking world. Thank God. If it ain't broke don't prefix it. There, I couldn't resist and this story is already twenty words too long.

Coach-Class to Charlotte

US airlines employ the oldest air-hostesses. This is both quaint and not a little sad, that they keep them up in the air that long. Mostly quaint, revealing a paternalism in American corporate culture that is surprising. A facet we as outsiders have overlooked, lost amongst all the bad stuff, like asset-stripping, outsourcing and general corporate raiding.

Unlike the bimbos on Virgin, all visible panty-lines, rustling stockings and wafts of contemporary perfume, U.S. airlines' hostesses have no sense of fashion or style. This extends to the airline itself, in toto. They aren't crippled by a desire to be contemporary. The styling, the seats, the folksy service, right down to the graphical layout and interface of the entertainment system menu, all harks back to a previous age. Nostalgia without anxiety.

The southern, Georgian, if I'm not mistaken, accent of the middle-aged black woman who greeted us and proceeded to seamlessly inform us of their current credit-card/air-miles tie-in with Bank of America, was so thick, so ethnic, so unselfconscious, that the vast diversity that such a country contains, encompasses, and in some way takes for granted, is again surprising. On this plane, and other American carriers, you chance upon a quietly confident everyday America, at ease with a diversity of ages and ethnicities.

The cadence and diction of this woman's voice, albeit reading haltingly off a crib sheet the details of introductory interest-rate offers and how many points one would earn for so many miles, this voice could have been heard in another century.

Or so it made me think as I listened to her. Thinking back, perhaps this delivery was a little forced, if not to say desperate. A bit like the rising inflections of the game-show host in *The Hunger Games*.

But back in the moment of settling into my chair, taking it all in, the words, the turns of phrase used by these air hostesses, attentive yet oddly euphemistic, sound like they come from another era.

Take for example the American word 'cocktails'. A word which celebrates the contents of a wet bar. A phrase doubly nostalgic, containing both a memory of the illicit pleasures of prohibition, yet also evoking the more recent post-war optimism of the triumph of a certain kind of civilisation.

I channel a tipsy Cary Grant as I sip my vodka and tonic. Lounging, laconic, lighting a cigarette with a gold lighter. Him not me that is, eventually and fatalistically slugging back his 'Vodka Tonic' in expectation of the next. The omission of the 'and' somehow focuses us on the drink's cocktail nature. The lacuna performs a runic function on my drink, transforms it into my cocktail of choice, one of the Brahmin liquors.

A word at home in both the age of luxury ocean liners and the aeroplanes that imitated and replaced them. 'Cocktail hour' conjures barmen in Fezes under the blades of ceiling fans, in the hotels and clubs of Cairo and Tunis, the colonial privilege of cold drinks in hot places. The tinkle of ice in short glasses and the fizz of champagne in tall ones. Gimlets and Bourbon, Manhattans and seasonal Eggnog. Chivas on the rocks.

Also drunk by the suburban denizens of John Cheever's dark, smouldering stories, which read like the flip-side of so much civilisation, an essential counterweight to the necessary failures and compromises of suburban living. Cocktails, the 1950s; the redemption of little Catholic promises-to-self at the end of each day, made upon waking.

When the drinks trolley comes around again I ask for a tomato juice and get a legend. 'Mr. and Mrs. T's Famous Bloody Mary Mix.' Every time I fly US Airways I am looking forward to its savoury snack even before I pass security, and re-reading the side of the can which actually advertises a website celebrating the

American art of tailgate parties (www.mixitup.com). Its promise lures me through security, the ritual taking-off of shoes, socks, nearly as embarrassing as underpants, the un-snaking of belts, the debagging of laptops, all just hurdles I have to jump in order to quench my thirst with somebody else's nostalgia.

Tailgate and supper parties, both echoes of a culture at a higher point than now in the arc of its rise and fall. Remnant words like the abraded standing stones of a once-great civilisation that litter the countryside, still pepper the language; names of long-derelict castles and feast halls, their stones borne away for other more pressing if prosaic purposes. Tales of the art of war and the formal exchanges of an elaborate court diplomacy resurface in an age of mud and hunger.

Reminders of when we hit the ball at the top of its bounce, when we were at the top of our game. I hear in the voices of these ancient air-hostesses the lingering rhythm of a supreme confidence and optimism that to an outside observer seems other-worldly. Words that have become totemic in the space of a mere fifty years, freighted still with the elaborate connotations of a persistent cargo cult.

But who is this detached outside observer? Not me, as I sip my spicy tomato juice and crunch my chive and onion pretzels, not me.

There is also a ubiquitous kindness about the service on these planes that mindlessly gnaws away at the world of terror and disenchantment. A formal 'have-a-nice-day' politeness that is the gateway to a more genuine concern.

I heard one hostess take an elderly Anglo-Indian woman through her immigration forms, because she couldn't read English, without a hint of condescension or impatience. She read out the questions on the customs form for the woman to fill in, one by one: 'Have you been in contact with farm animals recently?' The woman was visiting her daughter in Charlotte, I had seen her wheeled onto the plane at check-in. I don't want to read too much into this, but the absence of any implicit racial/cultural superiority in this exchange did surprise me.

I was sitting next to a young Muslim woman, who at six o'clock took off her earphones (she had been enjoying *Pirates of the Caribbean: Dead Man's Chest* on the seat-back screen, whilst eating her special meal) and sat quietly with her hands on her knees, head lowered and keened back and forth ever-so-slightly as she offered prayers. I was looking at the photograph of a topless model in the *Daily Star*. I closed the paper surreptitiously and wondered if the plane was facing Mecca, as I watched her out of the corner of my eye. Later we had a small conversation; she was studying marketing at a university in Virginia and spoke in an American English that employed the same phrases and pleasantries as all the other Americans that surrounded us.

Slight turbulence. The overhead lockers rattle on their central spine, looking to shake themselves free and kill us all. Brace. A cascade of perfume and liquor. Brace. Death by duty-free, killed by our own hubris. Brace.

My neighbour's face tenses slightly, before returning its gaze to the screen and relaxing. Inshallah, we shall both survive this flight.

These planes are old, bits falling off them, broken trays, ripped stitching, all dutifully entered into a manifest for future repairs. None of the gadgets look modern. America is the nation state expression of Microsoft Windows. Windows the software expression of a certain type of America. The type that runs US airlines. I fiddled with the screen. The drop-down boxes that appear when you click the Start button are unprepossessing to say the least. They are forever 1988. Toolbars that only acquired the ability to go translucent with Windows Vista in 2007 for Christ's sake! But I like this. This uncoolness. It also extends itself to how middle-America dresses. Especially dresses to travel. Comfort over style, accommodation over cut. But is there an arrogance to this, an obese swagger? Who cares what we look like, we rule the world? Would lazy gods smooch about in tracksuits, hoodies, baseball caps, Ts, the older ones looking like pampered daycare/spa patients? I never saw Colonel Kurtz wearing a suit. Is there an implicit insult to other cultural sensibilities in this informality? I think again of the conservative/ immaculately dressed Muslim woman sitting next to me, habitually tucking her hair up under her headscarf.

The fatness and girth of these people, whose size demands clothes with elasticated waistbands and drawstrings, the Gargantuas and Pantagruels of the Midwest, feasting in a deracinated land of Cockaigne.

Up-close and personal I experienced all these contradictions. I felt revulsion but also wanted to be accepted by this strange otherworldliness. America still has this ability to wrong-foot one's assumptions. It's all about the money, stupid, yet at the same time it isn't. When we landed it was night and a fire engine circled the plane hosing us down with water, its siren blaring. For a beat I nearly shit myself. My neighbour pressed her face to the window, turned to me and shrugged. An announcement came over the tannoy telling us we were all lucky to be on-board the last flight of air attendant Gale Jordan, who had given thirty-three years of service to US Airways, flying over 60,000 hours. The fire engine was part of the welcome committee, an honour guard from her home base of Charlotte. Everybody started clapping and Gale blushed. The Muslim woman clapped and smiled at me. My hands stayed palms down on my knees, I keened forward a little, praying to my own personal, less literal Mecca. The sentence 'On a wing and a prayer' popped into my head as Gale openly wept in the aisle. Under the layers of pancake and blusher that had protected her skin for the last thirty years I saw her face struggle to colour and tears well up and spill over her mascara, taking much of it with them as they cascaded down her cheeks like so much alluvial silt. She looked like a played-out hooker. I felt terrible. As we got off the plane we passed a banner greeting Gale, and a gaggle of family members waiting for her to disembark. They clutched helium balloons, which eased them up on their toes in expectation. This duty, her career, a life celebrated by family, co-workers and fellow Americans. 'Go Girl!' and 'Love you Mom' rang in my ears as I walked to customs. The banner read: 'Mom, happy retirement, we love you! Go Gale Go.' I glanced behind me as I hurried past. Gale was coming up the ramp held up by her captain and crew. The Muslim woman was nowhere to be seen.

They bore Gale up into the terminal on a wave of celebration that made me feel ashamed of myself for hating them.

Welcome to Charlotte.

SWIM/SWIY

'SWIM couldn't make this up. The Jewish-princess advertising-agency producer from LA being wanked all over by some black guy on the dance floor of a Greensboro' nightclub. And if SWIY don't laugh then SWIY ain't human.'

A lot of America looks like the set of *Dawn of the Dead*. Urban spaces that could 'stand in for' the locations of seventies zombie movies. A lot of America is an experimental remake of those films, an installation in honour of them. A broke-down zombie-world fair. Somebody call the Doctorow. Ramshackle downtowns, deserted sidewalks, a surfeit of cars parked haphazardly, looking abandoned more than they look parked. Broken pavements and boarded-up shop fronts, liquor marts that spill their customers out onto buckled tarmac, into aimless-seeming traffic, lethargic suburbias, past shuffling homeless guys peddling flick knives. Everything seems to be designed for more people than there actually are. Vast parking lots servicing empty office blocks. The energy of commerce seems to have leeched away from so many of these places, leaving the punch-drunks of post-empire capitalism, or whatever we call it now, high and dry, in the closing-down sale version of where they really used to live.

Everybody must go!

Towns with burger joints that once again sell French fries, the faded word 'Freedom' still visible on the whiteboard underneath the more recently inked 'French'. Or the other way round depending on when SWIM wrote this story. The thought bubble 'French freedom' just confuses matters.

Soda fountains and pinball machines, coleslaw and refried beans. Crab shacks, Bojangles, Sizzlers and Denny's. Jack in the Boxes and Waffle Houses. Residual franchises from middle-America's middle ages.

Years ago I was in Corpus Christi shooting some commercials for the Texas and Mexico supermarket store chain H.E.B. The 'spots' featured dancers dressed as staff starring in a Broadway musical parody. The dancers were themselves Broadway/off-Broadway wannabes and the choreographer I seem to remember was the same.

H.E.B. started out as a one-store family business in Kerrville, Texas in 1905, owned by Florence Butt and her son Howard E. Butt. Now it's one of the largest food chains in America. That's a story with direction, the arc of a mini-series. It has shape, you can see where it came from and where it went, and the 75,000-odd people who work for H.E.B are part of the cast of where it's going. In many ways H.E.B is a redoubt against the inertia, the haphazard parking, the topological aimlessness of post-empire capital. Everybody gotta eat, right?

I took a walk down an empty main street, so deserted that it made you think about what the word main meant, in the sense that if the other streets weren't so important, were in fact subsidiary roads to this one, then what the fuck? This low-grade gibberish passed through my mind as I jaywalked across the deserted road.

'You should see this place during spring break', is what the guy in the empty tattoo parlour said. I can't add to this sentence, it has a terminal velocity all of its own.

I wanted to get a tattoo in Corpus Christi, in the hope that somebody would say to me one day, 'Where did you get that done?' and I could shoot back, 'Corpus Christi, Texas'. Which sounds cool, but I had no concrete idea of what tattoo I wanted and for some reason no inkling to sit still for the time it would take.

We were staying at the Omni and the tattoo parlour was opposite. I tried to focus on the tattoos in the window, challenged myself to like one. I liked the skeleton head in a cocked and crushed velvet top hat, it had a cool thirties feel to it, very

'Carnivale', with a drooping black cheroot clenched at the side of a broken jaw. I free-associated a mash-up of the Depression and Neil Gaiman's book *American Gods*. Echoes of what made this place, where it came from, had a traction that made the day intelligible, in the same way that thinking about Kerrville did when shooting in the H.E.B store.

The half-life loops of age and death fizzle as background noise, but I'm too old for a new tattoo and I left Texas unscarred, yet only after many lap dances with a half-Cherokee stripper, pitted skin and raven eyes smoke-signalling illicit pleasures under purple UV lights. Her mom looked after her son whilst she worked the pole. I wanted to call her 'Lap dances with wolves'. I promised to make her the heroine of a novel, the star of a movie. In my mind I toyed with the word 'breed', and imagined us smoking meth on the steps of her trailer as a wolf howled from the elevated height of a distant mesa and we disappeared in clouds of vapour, blowing meth into each other's mouths whilst everything twisted and coloured, a green-tinged white/Indian-trash version of the northern lights.

A cord of dense white meth-smoke snaking between us, one sucking, one blowing, you couldn't tell which way the smoke travelled. A Caravaggio moment that deserved to be honoured in rich oils.

We finished shooting in Texas and made our way North East. United, American or Delta got us out of there, and in no time at all we were in the Carolinas.

In Greensboro' I take it that there used to be a big furniture industry. 'American handmade furniture', say the signs of the few shops on the highway coming in, white-painted rocking chairs and 'Little House on the Prairie' tables slung outside under the signage.

Furniture as so much else has been replaced by food franchises along these empty highways. A line-up of ethnicity, a refraction of American immigrant dreams and promise of plenty from each. How can there be so many places to eat, that are mostly empty yet fully staffed, and that stay open regular hours? What kind of business model is that? What magic is at work? What strange mutation of capitalism allows this to recur across a whole continent? A supply-driven economy without hope of return? Where do the wages come from to pay all of the Americans that work in the food service industry? The waste, the food thrown away. Food cooked and prepared constantly in a cycle of production that isn't even predicated on the hope of custom.

Hungry, we pull into a Chinese restaurant, whose decoration caught our eye; a red dragon balloon/kite hybrid blowing in the wind, a pagoda-shaped building shell, painted bright red and tooled with gold. The surprise of finding ourselves about to eat Chinese! Because hung-over Chinese always sounds a great idea and SWIM actually, tragically, salivates at the prospect.

Inside we were met by a huge fish tank. These were display fish, not for eating. Pets of a sort. Fish that perform a display function whose meaning has been eroded beyond the point of salvage in this particular establishment. One of them had whiskers.

It brings to mind another trip, another town, another restaurant. 'Fishbones' in Orlando, where the menu once offered me salmon, line-caught by Sven Larsson at a depth of 330 feet, off the coast of Norway, less than a week ago. I forget the name of his boat but that was on the menu as well, in italics. He then proceeded to rattle off the specials. That night I ate the steak, and dreamt about Chilean sea bass ('Chilaayan' in American English when offered reverentially by the waiter as his favourite special).

Coming back to myself in the Chinese, as we are led to our seats I spy cigarette butts at the bottom of the fish tank. Lucky momentos of those who forgot to stub out at the door.

We go for the 'All you can eat 5.99 lunchtime buffet'.

A hundred trays under hot lights; deep-fried oysters, salt and pepper squid, a hot and sour soup tureen, opiated customers waddling and scooping up and down the three aisles of food, refreshed back in their booths by infinite refills of coke, topped up without question or answer by dumb waiters who are themselves customers. Chinese-food junkies waiting tables until they feel hungry again.

We were in town to shoot some spots for 'Goodies' headache powders.

That night, it was a Friday, we eventually discover a busy place. You can get loaded everywhere in America, everywhere is stocked, it's just finding the company that's difficult. Despite it being a sports bar with huge TVs on every wall we rush in, having narrowly missed inertia dining at the empty Olive Garden in the adjacent lot. The place was packed. Blue-collar folks both black and white, together but separate, a colour for each table, pitchers of beer and hot wings the only shared currency.

Earlier we had been across the road to a single-screen mall cinema showing *Resident Evil*, with tickets that were hand-torn. Behind a cordoned-off area an inexplicable model of a grand piano with life-size dancing figures next to it. Forties characters, maybe even meant to be Fred Astaire and Ginger Rogers, and on closer inspection of the plaque they were indeed 'Fred and Ginger', and again I am left with the absence of what this means, for surely it meant something once even if it doesn't now. Another when to help us with the why. Whoever put it there had to have a reason, had to have thought it was a good idea at the time. I got it as I filed past on my way to the auditorium. Eureka! The cinema was an outpost, an embassy, a consulate, however remote, for movies in general and Hollywood in particular. A national promise. I flash on Curly's wife in *Of Mice and Men* and her dustbowl fantasies of Broadway. Today, and here, it offered three-dollar movies for black teenagers on dates. And surely that was good enough and I should shut my mouth.

The next day we go on a location scout.

From the front passenger seat of a six-litre hybrid pick-up truck, my mind conjures a tragic and majestic history. 'The South' in all its terrible glory. Filling all the gaps, joining all the dots of the present, painting a faded yet pungent portrait of then, its canvas the alluvial flood plain of history.

Tobacco country. Cotton Plantations. William Tecumseh Sherman and his army marching through the South tearing the place up. Asheville, Rayleigh, Columbia, Savannah, Atlanta. 40 acres and a mule. Southern states put to the torch and to the sword.

Winston-Salem. Had it once been two places that decided to hyphenate themselves at a raucous joint town meeting once upon a time? How close was the vote? Famous cigarettes named after towns, or in some far-flung future archaeological fuck-up the other way round. This is the place for cheap cigarettes, the local industry more of a source of pride than a health hazard. Same as Steel-Town America, West Virginian Coal-Town America, Motor-City America, King-Crab America and on and on. Having a job, making something, being freighted with more meaning here than anyplace I have ever visited. As was being out of work. Woe to that guy. This I know has more dire implications than anywhere else, way beyond having money, earning the means to survive, to provide, it's identity that is at stake. Look at Team Detroit and all the rebranding they're trying out there. SWIM and SWIY had better watch out.

In this part of the world smoking is patriotic. Cigarettes are bought by the carton. We pulled into a low-slung convenience store sweltering on its own patch of asphalt. Cigarettes and alcohol, a stack of TV dinners, some frozen steak. A skinny Korean guy propping up his own counter, his fat daughter somewhere stacking shelves. A certain tension could be felt under the blanket of unsatisfactory air-con. My movie-polluted mind imagined an invisible shotgun under the counter, the

Korean guy's hand twitching over it every time people enter his store. Two black men slide up and down the aisles. We picked up some waters to a nod from behind the counter and went back outside. An abrupt exchange of cooled air for honest-to-goodness heat. For this was June and it just hung in the air, beating us back into our cars.

Back at the hotel, another Omni, I sat in a meeting room, one of those spiteful event rooms that hotels have in abundance, from where you can 'run a production'. It has wireless internet, we brought in a printer. It had the inevitable name, the Elgar Room, invoking a level of creative excellence I knew we would never attain even with our best efforts. We sat there, I next to the client, a friendly fat black woman in her mid-thirties, discussing the new packaging for the headache powders we were going to be advertising. In the commercial we had to show how ingenious it was. Our 'pack shot' would consist of the new 'tear', which was a line of perforated paper, along which the customer could tear off the top of the sachet. This product had always been sold in a wrap of paper, virtually identical to that which encases most grams of coke. I kid you not. Like in a nineteenth-century pharmacy where powders would be dispensed in such an old fashion by a man with moustaches, in twists of quality paper. There was an authenticity in this method of packaging that has since become contemporary.

The new packaging replaced this coke wrap with a cylindrical sachet that tore along an already perforated line at one end. This is what you 'take to the head' as the client informed me. I tried it and spilt the powder all over the table. My God I was far from home. The client's nails were long and perfectly manicured, they curled over the end of her fingers, flashing me back to a nightclub twenty years earlier in southern Spain where a dealer chopped out a gram with the thick curly dirt-black nail of his pinkie, shovelling the gear onto a glossy triangle scissored from a porn mag.

Those perfect nails, her imperfect body shape, the fact that the phrase 'nigger nails' bubbled into my mind unbidden, the powders we were selling, the stupidity of having to film the 'tear' in close up, the heat outside and the cold sweat of being indoors, all gave me an inevitable headache.

Online, cold with the air-con on, stuffy and hot with it off, trawling the internet for post-wank entertainment I found an online forum for people with drug and sex abuse issues. I followed the threads for crystal meth abuse and the insane posts of somebody called SWIM. This guy was fucked up, had been slamming meth for six years and his arm had nearly rotted off from what I could tell. No surprise he'd lost everything, and there wasn't any Breaking Bad epiphany, if indeed there was one on that show I never watched it – well just one episode. I got up to turn the air-con back on, sat back down and realised I was late for my pick-up and hurried down to the foyer.

The hotel was popular for conferences and junkets, weddings and sales meetings, and was mostly empty from dusk till dawn, whatever guests they had dashing from room to car in the precious moments when day turns to night or vice versa. Sometimes the lift would be full of Pentecostal Adoption Conference delegates, proud white couples of middle age pushing handicapped black or Hispanic infants about in pushchairs, their delegate accreditation swinging to and fro from lanyards round their necks. Badges of their honour, proudly displayed. Other times there would be elderly folks all dolled up and coming down to the vestibule for a veteran's supper to be held in one of the ballrooms. They didn't look like they knew which one, these old marines, displaced these sixty years from the jungles and undergrowth of the Bataan Peninsula. They looked sedated, were slippered and pushed frames about, the atria and vestibules clearly inducing agoraphobia in the old, both men and women alike, who skulked along the edges, shying away from the huge bronze-effect water feature in the middle of the room. Old men outflanking each other on the way, hopefully, to their tables.

Elsewhere there was a huge thousand-person nightclub inside the hotel, but for the life of me I can't remember its name. It was a perfect film location, all neon lighting and gold balustrades, exhibiting the odd asymmetrical layout of the late seventies, stairs, bars, internal veranda, restrooms and multi-levelled dance floors.

No sneakers, smart-casual dress only, read the optimistic sign. Monday, Tuesday, Wednesday, the place was empty. God we could do with a few laughs after shooting perforated sachets all day, but the bars and restaurants of the hotel were manned by a skeletal crew of guests and staff. It was as if the guests were paid to impersonate guests, as a training exercise for the staff, who were all either very young or too old. We asked where all the people were, why the hotel had such a big nightclub. 'You come back Friday night and the place will be packed, upwards of eight-hundred folks in there.' Yeah right. A band was booked for that night as well, fuck it they would be playing to an empty room, in a spooky empty hotel. We slurped down tens of watered-down vodka tonics in a vain attempt to get loaded and went to bed.

Friday night was wrap night. The next day we would be off, the crew and agency dealt back to the airport like a busted hand of blackjack. LA, New York, London would reabsorb us, our absence having gone unnoticed from the vast streams of human traffic that strangulate the globe.

So we decided to check out the club, see if the barman's prediction would miraculously come true. In the bar the two agency creatives, constantly plugged in iPod guys, know-nothings, but pretty harmless, realised they didn't have any real shoes to get in the club. They found it hilarious to go to the mall opposite, to a thrift store in which they could buy some dead man's shoes and finger lint in the pocket of a dead man's jacket.

In the meantime the club was actually filling up. They would join us inside.

On set they sat behind their laptops all day, barely looking up at the monitor. The producer approved shots as they trawled the web for their next YouTube clip to steal for another gig, or slumped desultorily waiting for the 'you're fired' email to come through the firewall. Either way they didn't 'enjoy the shoot' other than the craft services, just hanging in there for the wrap party.

That night client, crew and agency were all pretty drunk by the time the club doors opened. I participated in the casual indiscretions Americans make at work, because so much of life is work, so where else is there to be indiscrete other than at work, and all this added to a sense of commonality, of bonhomie, as we poured in through the club doors. On the stage a white band played reggae and R&B covers to an audience that was ninety-percent black. Locals who were all intent on having a good time and letting their hair down.

Good times.

The cotton club in negative. I wish I could remember the name of the band, but I won't make it up for effect. I just forgot.

Good times.

So I sit at the bar with the female client, who is good company. We have some drinks and end up chatting with a few local women at a stand-up table. I buy a few rounds and enjoy the view. The next thing I know is the agency producer comes up to us shaking, her hands down by her sides, but away from her body as if she doesn't want to touch herself. She had been a little drunk but whatever had happened to her sobered her right up, you know that feeling, when your mind clicks to attention overruling your body, which is still full of booze. An enforced state of emergency, a physical curfew gives your movements a kind of brittleness. She gestures to her trousers which look a little wet and says that the guy she had been dancing with had ejaculated all over her on the dance floor.

We all laugh, involuntarily. She also laughs and then we stop laughing and say some odd things, trying to make a drama of the situation because that's what this deserves, or so we thought. We ask what happened. Somebody actually makes an AIDS joke. We laugh nervously, she does too, using the joke to laugh it off, loosen herself up enough to talk. She says she went for a dance with the guy, who held both her hands behind her back with one of his and pinned her to him, whilst the other hand went in his fly, pulled out his cock and wanked off over her. Now at this point I'm sniggering a little with the client, it's unbelievable that this has happened. The producer fills in the details, at no point saying that the guy was black, because in that club if he wasn't with our crew then he was a black guy. What do we do? Call the police, get them to close the club down? Yeah right, we'd get lynched. She doesn't want a court case, the guy's long-gone, she just wants to get out of her fucking trousers and burn them. She sees the humour in what happened. In fact the guy's friend dragged her away from him and took her to the toilets so she could wipe herself down. It isn't mainly spunk on her trousers, but the effects of the wipe-down. He must do this a lot; his friend must do this a lot too. The producer says hesitantly that if we do nothing then maybe the guy would end up raping somebody. The music plays on, people dance, the band plays on and it's hard for any of us to do something that will change that, without irrevocably altering the evening. Even she doesn't have the will to do that. At this point when we are all fighting our inertia, debating what to do, the agency creative, the one wearing the thrift-store shoes, becomes all white-boy irate and says, in front of his black client, and referring to the guy who had ejaculated:

'Fucking nigger.'

As if he was going to do something about it. I wanted the ground to swallow me up right there and then. A club packed with black people, and this check-shirted thrift-store shoe-wearing twenty-something punk says that. I burst out laughing, so does the client, we order more drinks. The 'creative' is hustled out of the club by his partner. I assume they will be fired or the company will lose the account. The producer is taken off to change her trousers. I stay and drink with the client. She drinks a lot and starts talking to me about invisible chains as a reason she doesn't date black men. I'm drunk by now and bone-tired, yet the nervous energy from the evening keeps me awake and I make my excuses and join the crew in somebody's room to continue drinking and talking about what happened. By the time I go to bed I am bored by this story, I don't care, have become desensitised to what happened.

Years before, a female friend who had amazing long pre-Raphaelite hair was on the tube in London and a bloke stood up opposite her and jerked off all over her face. She said it took ages to get it out of her hair, and that she had to cut some of her tresses off. She called him a fucking cunt and beat the shit out of him before the transport police could pry her off and arrest them both. That girl had balls, her name was Rowena. Last I heard she was working for English Heritage.

These are the two times this story has happened to me.

Now this other girl, from another hemisphere, if not planet, went to a black nightclub and danced with a guy who came all over her. She was blonde, from California, dancing with a black guy in a North Carolina nightclub. These facts tell a story, but is that what really happened? Perhaps SWIY made it up. SWIM was there and nobody saw her dancing with anyone. She was dating some rich European guy who paid her no attention and was always abroad. She loved to be the centre of attention, how better to do this than claim that somebody had assaulted her. Wars have been started for less. Thousands slaughtered.

Or was it all real? Why would Somebody Who Isn't You lie?

In another time-frame I flash on the agency creative with the dirty mouth having a big black buck strung up regardless of what he did or didn't do, but for who he was, for the twist of lint in his pocket. The skinny white young man's horse skittering at the edge of the circle of flame, sweating under his hood, struggling to hold up his torch with one hand and control his mount with the other, casting an erratic swinging black shadow at a shallow angle out along a country road.

Black spunk on a blonde body. Rivers of blood rushing down through history washing up on the dance floor of this damn nightclub in Greensboro', and I just had to be there getting splashed all over my feet. I really didn't feel like myself on this trip, I felt like I was just tagging along. If I had been me, in full possession of myself, then I wouldn't have felt the need to write it down.

Reading this back now it feels like all of this happened to Somebody Who Isn't Me, which is fine, because it will probably only ever be read by Somebody Who Isn't You.

Invisible Manoeuvres

Downtown Stuttgart is one big building site, especially around the train station that looks like it was built before the war, but wasn't. A large silver Mercedes logo rotating atop the tower of this slab of a building, laying claim to ownership of such an industrious city. Anyway it's coming down soon as they are relocating all their stations and railway tracks underground, to free up space for development. This caused a huge political row in this conservative city, leading to the mayor losing re-election and the Greens winning control of the city for the first time but with the caveat of having to implement a project the opposition to which brought them to power; the contracts for redevelopment had already been signed.

The first architect was sacked due to the projected over-spend and he, I assume it was a man, burnt his drawings in his office bin before clearing his desk. An emotional response as they must have been on a computer, or indeed backed up on a cloud service like Dropbox, infinite copies available at the click of a mouse. A tragic Ibsen-like gesture nonetheless that bears the retelling.

I digress.

An expensive Swiss water-pumping system has been commissioned to prevent the new underground station from flooding, because the whole of the city, which spans four valleys, is way below the water table. If the pumps fail for 24 hours the place floods. It's like the set-up for a cheesy disaster movie. I can picture a late-night security guard about to take a second bite out of his midnight sandwich, his mouth gaping, steaming thermos of coffee on the desk in front of him, noticing a red flashing light on some dashboard, which he first taps, then taps harder, then reluctantly puts down the sandwich, stands (heaves himself) up, looks around, before going to investigate 'the pumps', which the flashing red light indicates have stopped working.

Why do this to yourself? To your city? Build an ultra-modern, automated anxiety machine underground, underneath it all. Haven't we got enough to worry about?

I digress further.

I am staying at the Arcotel Camino Hotel right in the middle of all this construction. Right by the train station. The hotel is on a dual carriageway corseted by roadworks and temporary road signage. Arcotel are a chain of hotels. They are 'passionate hosts' according to their website. I think I've stayed in other ones, but I may be wrong, the logo, the stylised letter A, in burgundy, is familiar, perhaps in Barcelona. They always put us in these relatively cheap but functional places. I have no idea what 'Camino' means or infers appended to the chain name. It googles as the Spanish word for 'path', which means nothing in this context. I was put here because it's a good hotel for business people; clean, bright and has broadband wi-fi. An odd detail I noticed is that in the corridors the room numbers light up; green if you are in and a kind of burnt orange when you are out. Also, like so many corporate hotels these days, you have to use your room keycard to go up in the lift. So the businessmen have to come down to meet their hookers, which I imagine is awkward and probably puts some punters off. Hotels make me think of this kind of stuff, they take me down these type of dead-end story paths...

I no longer complain about keycards as opposed to real room-keys, they've gone, we have to move on. It's become pointless to mention that keycards don't work if there is any significant seismic activity. It would draw a blank from those behind the desk, those who unwittingly oversee another victory for progress and technology.

After a meeting I return to the hotel to fend for myself for the evening. I'm reading Curzio Malaparte's *The Volga Rises in Europe* and I take this down to the bar. I never usually drink alone but I order a local 'Schwartz bier' which comes in an authentic-looking Schwabian bottle and is dark, malty and delicious. It has that same pleasingly tactile white-ceramic metal-flanged stopper that Grolsh was known for in the nineties. I drink it and order another. To eat I order the house speciality, the 'Arcotel' burger. A lazy mistake, but it's only my first night, so you can put it down to 'first-night nerves'.

I drink and read.

Malaparte is there at start of Operation Barbarossa. I should say he's in on it, because for him it feels like a bit of a wheeze, which is I guess the fatal attraction of his work. He's reporting from Galatz, a Rumanian border town full of Greek traders, Turkish barbers, Rumanians and gypsies with finely kept beards and whiskers and its famous Eunuch horse-drawn taxi drivers. It's a bit predictable reading this book on a trip to Germany. I feel like I've been found out in bringing it, although I was reading it anyway beforehand, it wasn't a conscious decision at all.

The world Malaparte describes is so beyond my imagination that I google and wiki 'Galatz', slightly surprised the place actually existed and in fact still exists (on Wikipedia, information carries its own caveat) but am left none the wiser emotionally in how I feel towards this now-and-forever lost place and peoples. In fact I feel the same towards them, to the scene he describes, as I do towards the people of Tatooine in *Star Wars*. An exotic place full of colourful characters who entertain me in the immanence of their fictive reality.

As the war in the East begins (gets underway…), Malaparte is attached as an observer (dressed in his Italian Alpini officer's uniform) to a German infantry unit. He observes some Jews and Gypsies being arrested and remarks, 'I would not give twopence for their lives' as they are marched past him. No shit.

I put the book down next to my iPad and watch the flat-screen TV as I finish the food, the burger's dry morsels rolling around in my mouth, getting stuck between my teeth, point-blank refusing to go down until washed away by beer. They are showing a friendly between Germany and Argentina, the first since the World Cup. Germany are being soundly beaten. I order another black beer, one too many, as I start to feel tired half-way through drinking it, a little buzzed as the Americans would say. It crosses my mind that Di Maria is a good buy for Man United, the bastards, and then I drift off the game, concentrating on finishing my beer instead so I can go to bed. I pick the book up again. Malaparte is describing the Mongolian Soviet tank crews who are thrown against the German forces in the western reaches of the Ukraine. Counter-attacks and rearguard covering actions allow the orderly retreat and reorganisation of the main Soviet forces. The Mongolians operate tanks like they have ridden horses for millennia, individually circling the invading forma-tions of tanks and columns of men, riding round them as if still on horseback, tactics so similar to cavalry that the invaders call them 'Panzerferde' – armoured horses.

We have become mechanised I think as I swipe my keycard in the lift and ascend to my room. The Mongolians Tankists couldn't help but resist their mechanisation in the very process of becoming mechanised. Perhaps there is hope for us all, Stuttgart included, as I stumble down a carpeted corridor staked out on either side by green or burnt-orange glowing door numbers, a flimsy glider caught in the cross wind whilst attempting an illicit landing...

King Bun

Darts is all about mental maths. For the players, for the punters and for the bookies. What do I need to go out? What's a player's stats for each double, each treble? When to take a bet, when to stop, when to lay a bet off...

So when Marmaduke Brecon from the Jolly Sailor in Hanworth took on Jim Pike representing the Windmill Club for the *News of the World* Darts Championship in September 1938, it was about the sums. Back in the thirties 'in-game betting' meant a bookie or his runner taking bets from the home crowd and buying the opposing team drinks, whooping it all up and making a killing. Wet thumbs flicking through the odds, quickly pencilled in before the game. 1st leg 180s, highest check-out of the match, odds tumbling as the arrows mount up. More stats to process, the likelihoods of every outcome shifting columns invisibly with every throw, every pint sunk. Quick minds recalculating the numbers, and all the while, in the eye of this numerical storm, the players intent on figuring out what they need to go out, eyeing their favourite doubles, lucky trebles, in order to win each leg. Keeping a calm head amidst all the booze and the barracking when all about you are losing theirs...

Have a bang on that.

August 1938, Bermondsey

Georgie Boy Pallen, tired, his voice hoarse, but a tidy sum stashed deep in his pocket, sets off with an easy gait, his loose-fitting suit sailing him down the street. An uncomplicated night's work, the darts crowd not normally known for violence, so a night without tension, well, with less anxiety, because you never know, even when you know. Right?

Past midnight, three raps with the hand of a street door-knocker. Upstairs, a fleshy hand clamps the mouth of a startled-awake blonde, followed by up, and an ear to the door, expectant. Next a muffled shout, which sounds like, has the rhythm of…

'Open up, Police!'

Georgie Boy waits downstairs, smiling to himself, gyrating on his own feet, a young man, full of piss and vinegar, playing a prank on his boss with a twinkle in his eye.

Upstairs older eyes flick over the room, land on the spine of a big black ledger under the bed.

'Fuck me.' Wally mutters to nobody, 'Fuck me!'

He slips on his shoes, grabs the book, wipes the dust off it and chucks it out of the window. He girds himself, fag-end flicked on ahead, turns to the bed and shushes the blonde now propped up on one elbow. He winks, before turning back to the window.

'I'm too old for this shit.'

'Wally!' she screams.

He jumps, it's only a single storey, but he catches his foot on the sill and pitches forward. The railings go right through him, through his dirty-collared shirt, stuffing his off-white vest through his heart.

A big man, his body crumples over at least two posts, stone dead. Pages from the book came loose in flight, and now flutter down the street, wind pasting them up against lamp posts, tucking them away in gutters. Neatly spaced names and numbers filling every page, pencil smudging on contact with the wet gutter.

Georgie Boy sways by the door, chuckles to himself, a half-empty bottle of something swinging loose in his hand.

'Open up, Police!' a put on deep voice, trailing off, wasted as there seems to be nobody in. A last swig, a mumbled 'Well fuck you' as he walks off unsteadily into the night, the last we hear of him the now empty bottle smashing in the gutter. Under the window Wally's face has the look of surprise about it. Small details. The street lamp hadn't been working for more than a week. Silent surprise, he isn't found till just before dawn.

The blonde, framed by the window, knows better than to scream. She stifles a sob and disappears.

'Local bookie dead. Gruesome end for local character and illegal street bookmaker "Red Wally Sasso".'

Read the headline in the local rag.

'Who pushed Wally the Russian and what for?'

Read everybody's lips.

As if the threat of war wasn't enough to keep people occupied in the stifling heat of late summer. Local news, local celebrity. Tales of everyday life that offered some traction against the inexorable tide of history.

Hitler had nothing on Wally and Georgie Boy that August 1938. In Bermondsey at least, he had a lot of catching up to do.

May 11, 1937

The night before the Coronation all the women were out scrubbing the street. There was going to be a party, so it had to look smart; for the photographer, for the local paper, for the record. Georgie Boy came home to no tea, which pissed him off nearly as much as the fucking Royal Family did, his wife a mug like all the rest, so he went straight back out to the pub, muttering to the women he passed that the weather would be shit anyway so why bother.

Pint of stout, glass of port and brandy. Georgie got out his tobacco tin and rolled himself a fag, the habit calming him. Nobody bothered him when he was rolling. He lit up, orange flame sucked into the tobacco and opened his paper, *The Daily Worker*, breathed out and smoothed it out on the counter. At that moment, before any reading had been done, a small fella sidled up to him.

'Georgie?' A small hesitant man with a weaselly face, a rolled-up newspaper under his arm and a pencil in the top left pocket of his cheap suit. A punter. The top of the pencil looked wet, bitten.

He oozed the nervous energy of your everyday chump.

Smoke haze and pub silence hangs between them as Georgie takes his time reading:

'BUSMEN TO CONTINUE STRIKE'

'Yes, bud, what can I do for you?' His fingers tap out on his Players 'No name' tobacco tin.

He flicks the paper over to the back page, taps the headline.

'You hear? Mick the Miller just passed, made a lot of money out of that dog, a lot of money.'

Georgie is whimsical when slightly drunk, 'Mick the Miller' being a famous brindle greyhound who, as he says, had just died. He drains his pint in libation to the dead greyhound, pushes the paper sideways across the bar. The punter stares at it.

'Didn't have you down for a Commie Georgie.'

Georgie sobers, his eyes narrowing with unwanted focus, the little man draws back from the line he just crossed. All of this involuntary signs of the times, where the threat of violence was the coming currency. The moment passes.

'Cayton's the best tipster there is, Commie or not, you're the one should be reading the *Daily Worker* chump.'

The chump pushes the paper back across the bar, gets down to business.

'Last race of the night, what you give me for Highland Rum?'

'To win? Not a lot to be honest, lot of punters fancy that horse.' Georgie pulls out his pocket book.

'What about a forecast with Finnegan's Rainbow?'

'Better, can give you 3s, 2 for the reverse.'

'Straight, Highland Rum first.' Pencil-biter hands him a pound note.

Georgie nods, marks it down in his pocketbook. He looks at his watch.

'If you're going to the races I wouldn't wait on a bus, looks like the buggers are on strike.'

He winks, tapping his newspaper.

Georgie gestures for another round as the chump exits, his eyes smiling at that day's King Bun comic strip.

Later, nearby, Wally's office

Wally sweats over his books. In his late forties, and for somebody who came late to nutrition, he already looks a little dissipated. He stares as a blob of sweat lifts the ink off the page in front of him, magnifying the figures. He dabs at it with his finger, smudging it, making it worse. He pushes back from the desk in disgust and wipes his brow with a handkerchief. Head back, eyes shut, he sits there cooling. Which is how Georgie Boy finds him, momentarily defeated.

'You look like you been shot.'

Wally wipes the hanky from his face, eyes Georgie with his head back, fixing him in the crosshair lines of his face like a WW1 fighter ace.

'Well, I dodged the bullet. What do you know?'

He sits forward, pulls open the desk drawer, brings out a bottle of vodka and two glasses. From his jacket pocket Georgie pulls out a small fold of notes and a cloth bag of coins, places them on the desk.

'It's all there, average day, not a lot, a quiet one.'

He places the notebook next to the money as Wally pours them two glasses.

'It's the Coronation tomorrow, that's what it is. A fucking distraction.'

'And the women want the men to behave all right. Stay home, be sober. Pub was half empty.'

They drink as Wally counts the money and flicks through the notebook.

Georgie looks around the room. Could be a private detective's office, he thinks passively; a desk, a standard lamp, dirty window, blinds throwing shadows from the streetlight, some shelves, books. Not that he'd ever seen one except at the Troc-ette.

Ricardo Cortez starring as Sam Spade.

It was always one drink with Wally, never the bottle.

'I bet he's got a gun in that drawer.'

Wally puts the bottle back, Georgie Boy downs his shot, stands up leaning forward, fishing for a glimpse of that revolver. Wally slams the drawer shut and leans back.

It's definitely the blinds, slashing an orange glow across the room, that make it like a private dick's office, he decides.

'It will pick up, always does. Soon as things get back to normal.'

Wally is already copying back into his ledger the night's takings. Georgie stares at the book.

'Back to normal? What we need is a bloody revolution. Even the Bolsheviks paid their gambling debts Wally, remember that?'

'...and you in nappies at the time. You been talking to that kid Rubin again?'

Georgie Boy shrugs. 'The workers have nothing to lose but their gains.'

Wally smiles, hands Georgie Boy back his notebook.

'Smart arse. Commissar or king, makes no odds son, Jews like us, well, keep a packed bag under your bed Georgie, pub or no pub there will always be pogroms. Goodnight Georgie.'

'Night.'

Georgie has an idea, the booze birthing a thought, a way of fighting back, against what he didn't really care. He runs down the stairs. Wally twists his father's gold signet ring out of habit, gothic letters entwined. It's too tight to twist round his finger, it meets resistance; fat fingers, fat bulging up over the letters. A ring that in his youth had spent more time in the pawn shop than on his hand, but now he'd have to cut his finger off to pawn it again, so he better not fuck up. All this flashing through his mind for no better reason that Georgie Boy and his smart-arse comments stirring up memories, a mind more agile, thank fuck, than his body.

I feel nothing, no identity greater than me, no place other than the here and now. My kids, wife, work, that's who I am, everything else is a dangerous fantasy. Dad knew that alright, Frederick, Freddy, not even his real name, his Limehouse name he called it, stepping off the boat back in 1921. Got to use it for less than five years.

Wally balls his hands into big baby fists. He blows on the ink, like on a book of spells, pats his head once more with the handkerchief, opens the drawer and from deep inside, past the bottle, he pulls out an old oversized service pistol. He places it on the desk, his hands chasing sweat off opposite palms as he studies it.

'All I need is a Commie Jew for a runner.'

A lock-up, round the corner

Round the back of the flats was a lock-up garage. Georgie kept all his old shit in it, since before he got married. An old motorbike, too dirty to keep in the house, blah blah blah, but also other stuff; Georgie had always been good with his hands, mending, making, used to help his dad out at the allotment, built a trellis once for tomatoes and that took a lot of twine, which is what he was fumbling for now, a big ball of the stuff under the work bench in a cardboard box. That and the tin of white paint he never got around to painting the outside bog wall with.

Now it was late, everybody on the street tucked up for the big day. Painstakingly Georgie Boy, for he was nothing if not bloody-minded, painstakingly, he daubed the cobblestones. By the time he was done his suit, his one good suit, was ruined, covered in paint, but he couldn't care less. Next he threads the twine through the knockers of the doors on the street. Like lemmings he thought, we all got the same knockers, like lemmings. Made it easy to thread them all together.

All done, finally he tiptoes, and this for no reason other than enjoying the tiptoeing, anticipating the results of his mischief, across the street to climb up a lamp post. Perched precariously on the cross bar of the post, and with dawn creeping over the horizon, he fishes a half-empty bottle from his pocket, takes a big pirate swig and tugs hard on the end of the twine. Timing is all, as the morning sunlight illuminates his night's work.

Monkey-swinging from the post as the doors knock, and the women of the houses, for it's them who are already up, it's them who come grumbling out of their houses to find Georgie Boy Pallen, the youngest son of six boys and three girls to a local publican and wrestler, the youngest who always had to shout the loudest, grinning from ear to ear like the monkey he had been as a boy and still was, all covered in white paint.

'God fuck the King!' roars Georgie from the lamp post.

'God fuck the King!' in huge capital letters on the cobble-stones.

And the beating he got was fit for a king an' all. Husbands conjured from bed by the shrieks of their wives, stumble out into the street, knuckles rubbing eyes, they look up to see the culprit and the paint, and they swarm round the lamp post, swearing, shouting and grabbing for a leg.

'Come down here Georgie you commie bastard, you bloody Yid, you fucking mug.'

Georgie spits back, 'You fucking lemmings, you ain't worth the shit off my shoes.'

As he kicks out with his foot at their grasping hands, huge dockers' hands fishing for his foot, until they got him, pulled him down and beat him good and proper, until his wife beats them off, so as to get at him herself, lashing him with her tongue, her tears and her broomstick. The husbands skulked back indoors, but not before a round of, 'And fuck you an' all Georgie!'

Not least because he was right, not one of these men could give a fig for king, for country, for anything other than a quiet life and the pleasures of the pub, the whorehouse, and the track.

September 1938, Wally's office

Georgie Boy stood behind Wally's desk. He wouldn't sit down, but opened the drawer, gingerly took out the vodka. 'Shustov', the posh stuff, typical Wally. Georgie poured himself a few fat fingers and drank, then took out the gun, turned it over in his hand, felt its heft, sighted it, slid it into the back of his trousers like he'd seen them do at the flicks. He moved to the door but the gun dropped down the leg of his pants, so he had to take off his shoe to get at it, swearing, hopping, blood surging to his head as he bent down a bit pissed. Knackered now, Georgie wraps it up in the cloth, snatches the bullets from the drawer, and slams the door to his new office behind him.

Later, Lilliput Hall public house, Jamaica Road

The Lil, packed out, standing room only. Big men take up a lot of space. Stevedores, dockers, men used to wide arcs of space within which to work, handicapped by the cramped flats and busy pubs that cage them in their free time. The gaps filled in with narrow women, all hard work and disappointment. Georgie Boy sits with his brothers, their women, sisters and wives bringing them drink and food. He looks odd, demented, which is read by the room as grief. His father George stands behind the bar holding the whole place up and him five foot six.

The book, Wally's book, its pages all stuffed back together, sits on the table in front of Georgie Boy. Pathetic-looking, as if Wally's death had robbed it of something essential, not just the fact that it had been thrown from a first-floor window into a puddle, it pages thrown to the wind. He meticulously smooths out a page, a gesture of restoration, and reads from it. A big smile creases his face, a shock to some as up till now he has looked on the verge of tears. The book still retained the power of record. Georgie boy wonders what would have happened had he just burnt it.

'Last weekend's Police boxing championships. He'd take bets on anything.'

Laughs, cheers, all round.

He should have burnt it.

An old man shuffles into the pub unseen, only standing room right there by the door in the draught. And this man looks like he couldn't take many more of them, a lifetime of draughts, cramped doorways, etched into his face like so many IOUs.

'Jerry Collins had two quid on...'

And here he makes a show of reading a copper's name with both distaste and incredulity.

'...Sergeant Peter Rowley, to win by knockout in the third round. Do we know, apart from Jerry here, the policeman's friend, if this was the case?'

Sniggers, shaking of heads until a voice cuts through:

'I was there, my brother's a copper.'

This from a thin man at the bar, with a big voice, holding a pint, a tattoo across his knuckles, which reads 'FAST'.

'I'm sorry for that, but did he win?'

'He did an' all, soon as they took away his stool, he was up and laid the fella out. Third round.'

His other hand comes up, involuntarily runs his fingers through his hair as all eyes rest on him, the word 'HOLD' now apparent across the run of his knuckles.

'Huh, sorry I missed it. That's good enough for me, Jerry, here.'

Georgie, marks off the bet, counts the money from a pile of coins and roll of cash in front of him, spilling from a sack-like bag, its drawstring loosened. Jerry Collins steps up to collect his money.

The old man in the thinnest of suits which marks him out as a newcomer, a foreigner, makes it to the fire, the flames of which do not warm the reflection in his eyes. His profile almost that of a playing card, he stands, his version of sitting.

'And finally, Doris, says here you had an each way on Brendan's Cottage. Huh, backed that horse myself, not a large win but a safe one right my dear?'

'No such thing as a safe bet Mr. Pallen, you should know that.'

Her claw-like hands scrape up the money, a few coins and they disappear between what's left of her breasts.

The thin man at the bar rubs his hands one over the other, a faded blue-grey swallow graces the back of his hand, its shape rippled by veins like a flag in the wind. 'This fist flies' is the meaning of that, or perhaps if we find any other swallows on this man, then distance travelled by sea, probably under sail, if we remind ourselves of the 'holdfast' across his knuckles, which ages him, although his face is timeless in the dim afternoon light of this Bermondsey saloon bar in September 1938. 5000 miles for each swallow, I wonder how many we would find? Sailors and coppers, it must run in families, same as publicans and bookies.

All settled then, Georgie slams the book shut.

'The rest is vigorish, for the family.'

He slides the money back into the bag and pulls the string tight. The audience turns back on itself, loses focus and becomes a crowd, a busy pub crowd out on the weekend. In the back room a woman sits with two small children. She has been weeping, the kids, well, they laugh and play and why not. Georgie places the bag of money and the book on the table. The woman, late thirties, not suited to tears, looks at the money, weighs it with her eyes.

'And then what Georgie? When that runs out, what am I meant to do then?'

Georgie opens a silver cigarette case, offers her one and then lights them both. The time this takes allows for the return of some composure. They smoke, think.

'Marge is old enough to look after the little un' if I have to get a job.'

'I'll look after them babe, look after you. He said if anything should happen, he asked me to look after you.'

'You? Look after me? The fucking bookie's runner? Don't make me laugh. And don't call me babe neither!'

She smiles though, Georgie Boy too. Maybe there will be something between them, but not yet, not yet.

'Robin fucking Hood! Go on, urcha…'

This last through tears again, both of them standing too close to each other for this exchange to be read at face value.

Outside the Lil, New Year's Eve 1939

Georgie cups his ciggy, bends towards the shorter man, Alf Rubin, who lights him. Alf, aka 'Cayton', tipster for the *Daily Worker*, followed diligently by none other than the new Queen herself, that old soak and gambler, soon to be jeered and pelted with refuse on this very street.

Alf Rubin a small, sharp-on-his-toes Jew. A Jew with his bag packed, Wally would approved. Georgie spits, teasing a loose strand of tobacco of the tip of his tongue. He's in fancy dress, a cowboy with hat, neckerchief, checked shirt and full leather chaps.

'Hitler, he's got it coming alright', says Alf blowing out the match. They both smoke against the cold.

'That right King Bun? We've gone soft, since the general strike, mark my words, us lot up against the hun? This time round, who's your money on Alfie?'

Cayton shrugs. 'You want my tip? Read the paper.'

Georgie passes him his hip flask, Alf takes a swig.

'The Russians Alf? Is that what you want me to say? Half of them are in 'ere! No mate, Stalin ain't daft, they'll sit it out. Watch us get fucked, wouldn't you? Same as the Yanks. Sort Hitler out after he's knocked himself out.'

'I wouldn't be so sure, I hear…'

'You hear what? You gonna give me odds? Don't make me laugh. Anyway, it's freezing, you coming in?'

'With you dressed like that? Don't think so, I'm single Georgie, got my reputation to think of.'

'Right. Well then, happy hunting comrade.'

'Mazel Tov.'

Alf nods, walks down the street. Georgie tips up his wide-brimmed hat, bucks up his trousers, his chaps riding his hips like an oversized rubber-ring and whips out his pistol, sighting it on Alf's retreating back, shoots and blows imaginary gun smoke from the barrel before wading in through the pub's swing doors, this bitter New Year's Eve, that heralds nothing good for anyone.

Tower Bridge, December 8 1940

Georgie on another bloody shout, this time close to home, the shelter at the arches next to that bloody bad-luck pub The John Bull. Why on earth did they build a shelter there? For some reason he was the first down the stairs, gagged, threw up in his own hanky from the smell. Cordite and cooked flesh and burnt vegetables from the poxy greengrocers next door, stank like some sick cannibal supper. Fuck me, fuck me, fuck me, Wally was right the shit follows you, the stink, death, it knows you, sniffs you out, and it was sniffing here all right, pieces of bodies, like half a torso and whatever clothes it was in minced together, half man half fucking shirt, half kid half pram. He pulls on a pair of legs trapped under a block of cement, they come away without resistance, already severed from the rest, Georgie working by feel alone, his eyes so full of tears and smoke, his hands grabbing sinew and jagged bone.

Cut himself on a bloody bone he did, his small drop of blood adding to their gouts of it, a copper's whistle blowing for them to evacuate as the building was going to come down and he wanted then just to finish it, to be finished, to be crushed along with the rest, to have done. Bodies chopped in half, the rest, put better men than him in the nuthouse for life so why bother getting out? But in the middle of this, in all this, at the eye of this storm of feeling, flashes of thought and physical horror, Georgie hears a baby crying. A simple song that cuts through it all. His burnt and cut hands now wrapped in the clothes, the rags of the dead, he pushes over the body of a dead mother to reveal a baby gas mask, and a baby inside. He's not pulling on any baby legs not after what happened, but the whistle blows again, so he grabs the little diver, because that's what they look like in the gas mask, their little legs unprotected and open to the elements easy prey for sharks is what Georgie thinks, what flashes through his mind as he closes his eyes and pulls.

Eyes tight shut, tears welling out like pus from a wound, for he can't afford to see it happen again, pulls and the baby keeps crying his legs still attached to the rest of him as the gas mask comes away from the ruined cave of its mother and Georgie screams, makes a sound for the first time in what feels like hours,

'Here! A baby! Alive!'

He stumbles out somehow, into the fresh air. He gasps, eyes still shut and feels the baby being taken from him, his arms light, his hands sore and wet with god knows what and he thinks, he thinks, Wally I ain't gonna be taken here, buried like this, slick with the blood of women and babies, in a shit ARP uniform. He opens his eyes, he never saw the baby, but it doesn't matter, Georgie Boy for once knows what he's going to do next.

The Lil, New Year's Eve fancy dress party 1939

The old man, standing by the bar as far away as possible from draughts, but facing out into the pub, talking to anybody who would listen, if they could understand Russian that is, now his tongue had been loosened by the brandy and his eyes, well they have taken on a glow.

The old man's story, Moscow, 1917

We had a job that summer, human billboards marching up and down outside the Kremlin, embarrassing really but hey, it was money. Six of us like a walking card house, which was ironic seeing as that's where most of the money went. Straight down to the market in Khitrov, the Oreburka run card tables and bawdy houses, we couldn't help ourselves.

Advertising Shustov fucking vodka, another irony if that's the way you like to see things, Wally would drink himself silly on the stuff more nights than not. The whole deck of cards was about to come down, and I don't mind it if you think the metaphor is clumsy, because believe me I'm a simple man, and clumsy by habit, but walking up and down Red bloody Square as a billboard, well the humiliation at the very least was bound to cause an uproar if not a full-blown revolution in the heart and soul of a more modest man than myself. Wally, well he had ideas, when sober that is, ideas about how to set things right, and how to make the money to do it. You want to know about the last great horse race in Russia? Well, I'm getting to it...

Georgie Boy bursts into the pub, waving his pistol, rooting tooting, roaring with the booze and the blood up, inhabiting the costume, the wild-west energy coursing through his veins calling for the crack of gunfire and the smell of gunpowder, the sweat pouring into his eyes as he draws and fires above the bar, stumbles and fires again on his way down, catching the old man mid-story in the thigh and the whole place now hushed and Georgie Boy coming down as quick as he went up, as he gets up, sobers up.

'Oh shit! Sorry, fuck me, get a doctor! Somebody get a bloody doctor!' applying the tourniquet himself using the bloody paisley neckerchief that came with the costume.

The old Russian laughing now at something else, an unknown irony perhaps, thank God he's drunk thinks Georgie Boy, the strange old man who knew Wally, but arrived here after he died, sitting by himself, a face in the pub these last months, along with all the other incomers, the place overflowing, pouring what little money they had into Georgie's dad's pockets, this his family pub, him his dad's headache ever since he was knee-high to a Chinaman. His dad a professional wrestler who could spill you across the room with one hand whilst pouring a pint with the other without spilling a drop.

'George, Georgie Boy, when will all this palaver come to an end?'

Was about all he could manage, as the local quack dressed up as Abraham Lincoln opened his work bag and cut off the old man's trouser leg, the material so thin it tore with the smallest of cuts, after he had been laid out on the saloon bar by Georgie, now holding him down, the old man spluttering what remained of his story into his ear. After what felt like ages but was probably a few minutes, the doctor dug out the bullet, held it aloft to the drunken cheers of the crowd. Happy New Year!

Black Flag

2040

I had only known B for a few weeks, working with him in the kitchen garden of the open prison I had been sent to in 1985. I thought it was odd for an old man to call himself a letter, but didn't mention it, I was a few weeks from being released, so had other things on my mind. He had green fingers and the diet of the whole place benefited from them. His right-hand palm a mass of scar tissue he rubbed without thinking on cold mornings in the garden. He never asked me what I had done, and I asked him nothing in return. He had an accent, but spoke perfect English, somewhat old fashioned for I guessed he had learnt in in prison. We discussed the strike, the news, but as if on holiday and talking about local news, nothing that would affect us. So when I came to work and was told he had died it was sad, he was a likeable old guy with a funny accent, but nothing more. The fact that he had left me a box of notebooks and photos was more of a shock because of this. To be honest it was a bit embarrassing, I hardly knew the guy, but I can say it now, from the vantage point of my own exile and advanced years but the contents of that box, the scraps of hand-writing in Russian I didn't get round to having translated for years, changed my life.

1967, scrap of paper

After the war there were rumours that some Partisans in the Ukraine had raised the black flag and fought both the Red and the German armies. They had been Makhnovists, surviving members of Mahkno's very own black Sotnia. Nobody in history could have picked two more deadly foes. And how was this a rumour? Was it true, and if not who the hell would make it up? I can imagine in the Pripet marshes partisans could have fought under any banner they chose. A murderous anarchy already reigned. Had the flag laid hidden in somebody's cottage, under a bed, in a trunk, behind a sofa, stuffed there or neatly folded. Did any German officers remember the Mahknovishna? And again in '56, the flag again on the border with Hungary, the very end of this thirty-year war!

1921, notebook

We rode hard to the border. It was December. Frunze had been chasing Mahkno for weeks. We didn't speak for hours on end, for fear of letting the cold in. We came to a halt by a frozen part of the river that separated Ukraine from Rumania. The full moon, a steel ball bearing in the engine of the sky, lit up the snow as if it were midday. Mahkno, his wife Galina, Voline, a band of men numbering no more than thirty armed to the teeth but with barely any ammunition. What was left of his Sotnia, his bloody hundred. It was over.

Nestor pulled his horse alongside mine and draped his black flag over her haunches.

'She's cold. Take this. You will be punished no?'

'I never received those orders, the body of the messenger will attest to that.'

'So, where will you go? To Frunze? Throw the flag at his feet, the black flag of Nestor Mahkno, next best thing to my body, it may just keep you alive.'

'And you?'

'West. They destroyed my home, so we will find a new one. Mother anarchy loves her sons.'

'Black with our pain and red with our blood', I replied, tears streaming down my face.

'You'll probably be dead before I am, so don't cry for me Red Terror.'

He reared his horse, prompting a low-key whinny as he turned and trotted back to his men. A final flourish on home soil. I turned Mishka round in a more desultory fashion, pulling too hard on her bridle. The tears froze at the corners of my eyes, pain stabbing me there, in small punishment.

A week before, Mahkno had come to me in the middle of the night and for the first time amongst them I feared for my life. He handed me a bloody sheet of paper. 'Your orders', he grunted, before leaving me to read them. Lenin had ordered Rakovsky to capture Mahkno, and if not have him assassinated. Now after Mahkno had aided the Red army in defeating Wrangel, it was his turn. We had to consolidate the revolution. 'Or don't come back', Rakovsky wrote, 'Radek won't save you'. Outside the body of the messenger was already frozen by the well, a sign hanging from his neck. 'Bolsheviki.' I stuffed the orders back into his pocket.

And I rode away, I half-expected a bullet in the back, not from Mahkno, but one of the others. I deserved one and was to come to deserve many. Eventually I couldn't help but look back over my shoulder, but they were gone, all that was left were hoofmarks on the ice of the frozen river.

2040

In the murderous tempest that was the war in the east, the black flag had been raised. A promise fulfilled, an idea kept alive, to be passed on. An anarchist voice, however weak, raised in the face of other terrible hustings, a black flag haunting. Or was it all just propaganda? The enemy of my enemy is my friend. Sentimental, wished for, or a Nationalist backward-looking fiction. Backwards the new forwards. Whatever the case direction lends itself weakly to metaphor, left, right, back, forth. If we can escape that dead calm, that squall, that tempest going nowhere, then the black flag will fill itself with other winds. The Bolsheviks claimed the Anarchists were bandits and fought under the skull and cross-bones of the pirate. They were freebooters, marauders that should be hunted down like dogs. How much easier utopia in a boat, how easy to patrol your borders. I name this ship a free soviet, and to every man an equal share. And look who sailed in her, refugees, deserters, slaves.

In my hand I held the photograph he had left me along with his journals. A photo, black-and-white faded into flat-grey and milky-white. A folded ridge down its meridian, the image peeling back from the white cardboard. A cord of smoke twists itself around old trees. A wooden shack, maybe a trench running off into the forest. A group of men pose for a photo, arms raised to the sky clutching Kalashnikovs, curved scimitars. A scene from a film. An old hand-sewn banner unfurled behind the men, tattered but legible. 'Death to the palaces, peace to the villages.'

Crazy men, stout men in their forties and fifties. A few younger, boys, their sons or even grandsons. Leather jackets, black boots, long flowing hair. And there in the front row, almost sprawled across his comrades, a man with things tied in his hair, bracelets at his wrists. Not the dandy Partisan who singed the beard of Denikin? Tugged the moustaches of Wrangel? No, not the incorrigible Fedor Schuss? Surely he was dead by then? I'm tired enough remembering my own dead to carry these men and women gifted to me by B almost sixty years ago. Nobody cares for them, each generation has its own, our memories have to be freshly turned like cemeteries in order to function clearly. I take a match, to burn the photo, but it is damp, the flame won't take, I throw it into the fire instead, where it blackens but still doesn't take flame, instead it just stops being a photograph, dead matter instead, and finally ash. Fedor Shuss, Nestor Mahkno, Karl Radek and his half cousin whoever he was, B, agent Sasso, Officer Pyotr Semyonov, Prisoner number blah blah blah, Buba Sobelson, Sobelsohn, different names, aliases, titles, appendages, different languages with slight variations of spelling transitions between alphabets; nothing definite, nothing you can put your finger on, despite all of the facts that swamp us. His was a life like a photon! You knew where he was but not how fast he was going, or were dazzled by his speed with no idea of his location, by god the definition of Heisenberg's principle of uncertainty!

Heisenberg. Another story but not here, they, stories and I have to come to a rest.

We have lived in a time of soldiers and slaughter, uniforms and refugees. Of opinions, of starvation, of survival. A world of borders, of memory, the echo of horses' hooves, the silence of drones. The slash of blood on steel, the screams of the trampled, the silence of the survivors. I have seen Napoleonic graffiti on the bricks of London, Vietnamese villages brought to the high streets of our new towns. Northern villages bereft of pals, our boys in Iraq, in Afghanistan mourned in real time by mothers from Kent to Portadown. I have seen the horror of Royal Wootton Bassett, bodies strung from lamp posts, made witnesses to a thousand funerals. Six thousand crucified on the Appian Way, the living dead sealing the triumph of Rome for millennia.

We are Spartacus in this, our forever land of hunger.

Contemporary culture has eliminated both the concept of the public and the figure of the intellectual. Former public spaces – both physical and cultural – are now either derelict or colonized by advertising. A cretinous anti-intellectualism presides, cheerled by expensively educated hacks in the pay of multinational corporations who reassure their bored readers that there is no need to rouse themselves from their interpassive stupor. The informal censorship internalized and propagated by the cultural workers of late capitalism generates a banal conformity that the propaganda chiefs of Stalinism could only ever have dreamt of imposing. Zer0 Books knows that another kind of discourse – intellectual without being academic, popular without being populist – is not only possible: it is already flourishing, in the regions beyond the striplit malls of so-called mass media and the neurotically bureaucratic halls of the academy. Zer0 is committed to the idea of publishing as a making public of the intellectual. It is convinced that in the unthinking, blandly consensual culture in which we live, critical and engaged theoretical reflection is more important than ever before.

ZERO BOOKS

Capitalist Realism Is there no alternative?
Mark Fisher
An analysis of the ways in which capitalism has presented itself as the only realistic political-economic system.
Paperback: November 27, 2009 978-1-84694-317-1 $14.95 £7.99.
eBook: July 1, 2012 978-1-78099-734-6 $9.99 £6.99.

The Wandering Who? A study of Jewish identity politics
Gilad Atzmon
An explosive unique crucial book tackling the issues of Jewish Identity Politics and ideology and their global influence.
Paperback: September 30, 2011 978-1-84694-875-6 $14.95 £8.99.
eBook: September 30, 2011 978-1-84694-876-3 $9.99 £6.99.

Clampdown Pop-cultural wars on class and gender
Rhian E. Jones
Class and gender in Britpop and after, and why 'chav' is a feminist issue.
Paperback: March 29, 2013 978-1-78099-708-7 $14.95 £9.99.
eBook: March 29, 2013 978-1-78099-707-0 $7.99 £4.99.

The Quadruple Object
Graham Harman
Uses a pack of playing cards to present Harman's metaphysical system of fourfold objects, including human access, Heidegger's indirect causation, panpsychism and ontography.
Paperback: July 29, 2011 978-1-84694-700-1 $16.95 £9.99.

Weird Realism Lovecraft and Philosophy
Graham Harman
As Hölderlin was to Martin Heidegger and Mallarmé to Jacques Derrida, so is H.P. Lovecraft to the Speculative Realist philosophers.
Paperback: September 28, 2012 978-1-78099-252-5 $24.95 £14.99.
eBook: September 28, 2012 978-1-78099-907-4 $9.99 £6.99.

Sweetening the Pill or How We Got Hooked on Hormonal Birth Control
Holly Grigg-Spall
Is it really true? Has contraception liberated or oppressed women?
Paperback: September 27, 2013 978-1-78099-607-3 $22.95 £12.99.
eBook: September 27, 2013 978-1-78099-608-0 $9.99 £6.99.

Why Are We The Good Guys? Reclaiming Your Mind From The Delusions Of Propaganda
David Cromwell
A provocative challenge to the standard ideology that Western power is a benevolent force in the world.
Paperback: September 28, 2012 978-1-78099-365-2 $26.95 £15.99.
eBook: September 28, 2012 978-1-78099-366-9 $9.99 £6.99.

The Truth about Art Reclaiming quality
Patrick Doorly
The book traces the multiple meanings of art to their various sources, and equips the reader to choose between them.
Paperback: August 30, 2013 978-1-78099-841-1 $32.95 £19.99.

Bells and Whistles More Speculative Realism
Graham Harman
In this diverse collection of sixteen essays, lectures, and interviews Graham Harman lucidly explains the principles of

Speculative Realism, including his own object-oriented philosophy.
Paperback: November 29, 2013 978-1-78279-038-9 $26.95 £15.99.
eBook: November 29, 2013 978-1-78279-037-2 $9.99 £6.99.

Towards Speculative Realism: Essays and Lectures Essays and Lectures
Graham Harman
These writings chart Harman's rise from Chicago sportswriter to co founder of one of Europe's most promising philosophical movements: Speculative Realism.
Paperback: November 26, 2010 978-1-84694-394-2 $16.95 £9.99.
eBook: January 1, 1970 978-1-84694-603-5 $9.99 £6.99.

Meat Market Female flesh under capitalism
Laurie Penny
A feminist dissection of women's bodies as the fleshy fulcrum of capitalist cannibalism, whereby women are both consumers and consumed.
Paperback: April 29, 2011 978-1-84694-521-2 $12.95 £6.99.
eBook: May 21, 2012 978-1-84694-782-7 $9.99 £6.99.

Translating Anarchy The Anarchism of Occupy Wall Street
Mark Bray
An insider's account of the anarchists who ignited Occupy Wall Street.
Paperback: September 27, 2013 978-1-78279-126-3 $26.95 £15.99.
eBook: September 27, 2013 978-1-78279-125-6 $6.99 £4.99.

One Dimensional Woman
Nina Power
Exposes the dark heart of contemporary cultural life by examining pornography, consumer capitalism and the ideology of women's work.

Paperback: November 27, 2009 978-1-84694-241-9 $14.95 £7.99.

eBook: July 1, 2012 978-1-78099-737-7 $9.99 £6.99.

Dead Man Working

Carl Cederstrom, Peter Fleming

An analysis of the dead man working and the way in which capital is now colonizing life itself.

Paperback: May 25, 2012 978-1-78099-156-6 $14.95 £9.99.

eBook: June 27, 2012 978-1-78099-157-3 $9.99 £6.99.

Unpatriotic History of the Second World War

James Heartfield

The Second World War was not the Good War of legend. James Heartfield explains that both Allies and Axis powers fought for the same goals - territory, markets and natural resources.

Paperback: September 28, 2012 978-1-78099-378-2 $42.95 £23.99.

eBook: September 28, 2012 978-1-78099-379-9 $9.99 £6.99.

Find more titles at www.zero-books.net